NO LOVE TO DIE FOR

A Janis March Mystery

Sharon Anson

CONARD HADDOCK PUBLISHING

ISBN: 979-8-9866306-4-9

Published by Conard Haddock Publishing LLC
ConardHaddockPub@gmail

CHAPTER 1

My name is Janis March – named after Janis Joplin, who was a friend of my Great Uncle Chad. I grew up in Sutterton, a town about two hours southeast of Chicago. I still live there. After high school, I attended college in Vincennes, studying mostly forensics. With two years of college under my belt, I was pretty sure I could qualify to join Indiana's state police force. At the time I was on the force, women officers were almost as scarce as hens' teeth. That's why I left after a few years. But I have been, for some reason I've never quite understood, always obsessed with crime. So, the next step in my journey through life was to become a town cop. I worked my way up to detective. Then got out. I was tired of being bossed around.

Now I'm a P.I., somewhat flamboyant, long auburn hair, quite good-looking, if I do say so. Still turning heads at 38. I've been married twice. Both times to losers. One ex now lives in California with a sixteen-year-old, and the other is in the Indiana State Prison for armed robbery.

So I live with my mother. I like Mom. It's a good life. Mom says to me once in a while, sadly, that someday she'll die and leave me her house and a lot of money. With the emphasis on "a lot" because my mother is descended from a robber baron who flourished in the early 1900's. My mother's house – in which I grew up and in which I now live with her – was built by the son of said robber baron, a son who left the East and, for reasons now lost in time, chose to build a stately home on five acres in Sutterton. The house is in the Tudor Revival style. It has eight bedrooms, a library, an indoor pool, an outdoor pool, a marvelous playroom I utilized extensively as a child. The playroom has at one end a full-size stage with the original, but still beautiful and intact, blue silk stage curtain. A six-car garage was added at some point, along with a guesthouse that has a living room, a dining room, three bedrooms, two bathrooms and a kitchen. A cousin once told me that Wendell Willkie and his wife stayed in the guesthouse for several weeks after he lost the presidential election of 1940. This beautiful guesthouse is now my office.

The big house and its attendant buildings and grounds require a lot of care. Although my mother does her own cooking, she often spends her days standing in the kitchen like a traffic cop sending various providers of domestic care – roofers, gardeners, pool guys, cleaners, waxers, polishers – in the right directions. Then, of course, she must judge their work, hopping from garden to garage to bedroom to swimming pool. I love Mom but if anything were to happen to her, I'd sell the house and the rest of the real estate (I don't want to be a traffic cop) and escape to Mexico or Los Angeles. I'd like Mexico or Los Angeles. I would love adventure, life in a place that is not Indiana, a place that holds surprises for a girl brought up in a small Midwestern town. But for the present, it's me and Mom and my two border collies, Tam and Bud.

Crime. Yes, why do I care so much about crime? I've asked myself this question often. Simple felonies interest me somewhat, but I prefer especially bad crime. Especially murder. As I'm writing this, I'm thinking, well, isn't everyone fascinated by bad, bad crime? Maybe. Maybe not.

I usually think of people who are interested in bad, bad crime as those who have seen bad, bad crime and/or have lived through a bad, bad time. For me, however, that's not the case. Think on this: In this wonderful town of Sutterton, a town of approximately 30,000 souls, the only local murder I ever heard about when I was growing up was the killing of a female parole officer by one of her charges. This happened when I was about ten. At the time, I asked my mom, "How did he kill her?"

Mom said, "Don't think about that."

I said, "I am thinking about it."

She said, "Okay, he walked into her office and shot her. Are you satisfied?" I don't recall the rest of the conversation. It's odd to think back now about how, as a child, I had this idea that murder was extremely uncommon, that human beings did not often actually squeeze throats, shoot guns, slash with knives. I didn't understand that people commonly do this not only on TV (and then usually only in big cities), but also in real life. Yet I knew of only one actual murder in my home town the whole time I was growing up.

However, I think I must have had some inkling of the true possibilities of human violence and the snuffing out of life. When I was twelve, Butch Moore, an eighteen-year-old who lived about a mile away from our house, hanged himself in the basement of his family home. My mother said to me at the time, "Don't think about what Butch did." I had questions. Why? What for? Did he want to go to heaven before he got old? Never got any answers. And my mother's father, Dean, was killed in the Viet Nam War. Of course, he died long before I was born. Ran off to join the army, leaving behind a wife and child (my mom). He was an eager anti-communist. But then, everyone in Indiana was. And is.

I can't mention my grandfather Dean's name to my mom without her turning on the waterworks. Sometimes I join her, though I'm not sure if I'm sobbing over Dean, whom I never knew, or maybe sobbing for my father (for whom my mother would never sob). He was an attorney, a reliable man, got up every weekday morning and went to the office. He loved to quote the rich and the famous. Our love of those quotations was one of our bonds. And I remember everything he said. Whenever my mother was talking about her money, her guilt about having it, about her having done nothing to earn it, he would sometimes say, "Don't feel guilty, dear, about your money. Remember, as Eisenhower once said, 'Time disinfects dividends.'" Two years ago, my dad became sick for a month and then left this life as quietly as he had lived it. It was hard to lose him. He was my favorite person.

I'm addicted to the real-crime TV channels *Oxygen* and *Investigation Discovery.* In my down time, I binge watch these channels on the TV in my office. The story I'm about to tell begins with me sitting in my office, feet up on the desk, watching *Investigation Discovery's* "Evil Lives Here." I love "Evil Lives Here" because each story ends with the ultimate triumph of someone on whom long term pain has been inflicted. The perpetrator is always in prison or dead by the end of the episode. You get to see a late-prison or slightly-pre-death photo of the perp obviously in shambles. Justice has been done!

So today, it's "Evil Lives Here," but I turn it off when I hear the phone ring. The landline. Tom answers it. He's my assistant. 23 years old. Brilliant. Graduated from Purdue with a degree in computer science when he was 17. Like me, he lives with his mother. I think social interaction is difficult for him. When he took this job, he said he was happy to have a job in which he could use his strength – computer technology – but could also have the adventures of a sleuth. He bills the clients, pays the bills, answers the phone, and he's a true computer whiz. An assistant from heaven. And also, he cares, which is the reason I never listen to my mother when she says out of the corner of her mouth, "Dump him." I will not dump him. He's good to the dogs, too, and will run with them when I can't.

Tom yells to me that the man on the phone is a potential client who wants an appointment to see me. I yell back, "Tell him 3:00 o'clock." Three gives me enough time to finish my lunch and watch a few more episodes of "Evil."

I yell to Tom again, "Name? Issue?"

Tom yells back, "Johnny Cheung. C-H-E-U-N-G. From Melton. Wouldn't tell me the issue."

Tom hasn't been with me long. I get up and walk into the front room to Tom's desk. "Tom," I say. "You have to be able to get more information when people call. Marital issues? Kid has run away? Debt problems? You have to learn to get something. You have to turn on the charm a little. I don't like people coming in here about whom I know zip."

Tom looks up at me with his big, geeky, uncharming eyes. "Okay," he says, as if I'd beaten him harshly with a bamboo rod.

"Good," I say, and I go back to "Evil."

At three, no Johnny. At four, no Johnny. At 4:30, my mother calls to say there is a Chinese or Japanese or Korean man at her front door. She says, "You know I want you to tell your clients they're not supposed to come to the big house. It's irritating." My clients always go to the big house.

"Right, Ma," I say. "Tom will be right there." Then I watch Tom walk across the gravel toward the big house with his head hanging way too far forward, as if he wants to eat the ground. All I can think about then is how much I love Tom. So good with computers. His computer has already found two men named John Cheung who live in the Melton area. One old; one young. Both appear to Tom to be regular guys.

When Johnny Cheung enters my office, I realize he's the young John Cheung. Maybe 30 or 35. Tall, good-looking. No smile, however.

"Sit, Mr. Cheung," I say. He sits. He is clearly upset. Can't sit still. Jiggling this way and that. Hand wringing, in a way. Not real hand wringing. But something with the hands.

"My wife," he says. "She's missing."

"How long?"

"Four days. Since Friday"

"Have you told the police?"

"I'm Chinese. We don't tell the police anything."

"You're Chinese? You don't have an accent? Where were you born?"

"I was born here. Second generation. You don't understand. Second generation or one-hundredth generation, you're always Chinese. And the Chinese have as little to do with the police as possible. That's why I came to you."

"Sammy Teng must have sent you," I say. When I was a police detective, I once investigated Sammy Teng for a murder he hadn't committed. I knew Sammy liked me even though I was mean to him.

"Yes," Mr. Cheung says. "Yes. It was Sammy,

Ms. March."

I say, "Call me Jan."

He says, "Call me Johnny."

CHAPTER 2

Mike Taylor is a police detective, someone I used to work with when I was a detective. Since I left the force, he helps me with my business, mostly by giving me advice. We also go out; we dance; we sleep together. The sleeping together and stuff like that happen at his house where he lives with two twelve-foot-long boa constrictors. (My mother would think she were condoning evil activities if we were to sleep together at her house.) That's the reason I'm at Mike's, checking for the location of the boa constrictors, checking closets, closing doors. He lets the snakes, named Curly and Stretch, hang out indoors. I hate Curly and Stretch. Sometimes I hold Mike's pretty face in my hands and say, "Mike. Mike. Why boa constrictors? Why? Why?" He loves them. What can you do? As soon as I feel safe from being eaten by a snake, Mike and I kiss, drink wine. I tell him I want to run a case past him. Mike's not only a pretty face. He has great cop instincts, too. Much better than mine. When I was a detective, I always would say, "The husband did it." Then I would go home and drink a bottle of beer. (Just kidding.)

"Mike," I say. "Stop drinking for a minute. Listen. I need your help with something. I need you."

"Okay." He smiles. God, all those fabulous straight, white teeth!

"Yes, listen. I have this case. Chinese guy. Not really Chinese. Second generation. Financial adviser in Melton. Wife has been missing since Friday. He won't report this to the cops because he thinks Chinese and cops are not a good mix. Two children. Under age 10. Wife's 35. She's also second generation. Her name is Grace. Works part time with her husband in the financial practice. On Friday, she leaves work to go to the doctor. She's supposed to take her husband's car, which is sitting in the parking lot, see the doctor and come back to the office. But none of this happens. When she doesn't return to the office, her husband goes out to the parking lot. His car is parked there. Husband calls the doctor's office. Grace was never there."

"Well, your client is the husband. Knowing you, I'd think he'd be at the top your list of suspects."

"You're teasing me now. Don't do that. This guy didn't do anything. No. This is serious. I sense something awful about this."

"She ran away," he says, shrugging his shoulders.

"You're hopeless. I want you to take this seriously. I was thinking maybe you could come with me to Melton tomorrow, meet John Cheung, retrace steps, that kind of thing."

I'm worried that Mike's going to say that this should be a police matter, and that because it isn't, he can't do anything. But he smiles at me and says,

"Of course. Anything you want." Then he kisses my cheek lightly.

The next morning, the drive to Melton, an hour and a half away, is a bore. I'm thinking, as I'm racing along, that outside of bed and outside of work, Mike and I have nothing to say to each other. But I like him a lot, so maybe that's enough. My mother keeps saying to me, "Why don't you get married?" I assume this means she knows I sleep with Mike on the nights I'm not at home. Otherwise, she would say, "Why don't you find someone to marry." Right now, my state of mind is such that I don't think I could marry anyone. I have deep regret about the two bad husband choices I made in the past. I worry that I could never make a good choice. Mike's fallen asleep in the passenger seat. His head is back, snoring. I hate snoring.

We first visit the offices of Johnny's financial services company. Johnny has his own small office building in downtown Melton, a town much larger than Sutterton. The downtown area of this lovely old town is no longer teeming with foot traffic, as it once was. Retail shopping is now an activity carried on almost exclusively at malls near the town outskirts. It seems odd to be downtown. We drive by a few restaurants, some doctor's offices, a couple of antique shops, Johnny's office building. No more the little downtown dress shops my mother used to take me to when I was a child.

In the interest of full disclosure, when I introduce Mike, I tell Johnny that Mike is a police detective. "But he's with me here in a different capacity today, as a consultant." Johnny seems to be fine with this.

I see five people, in addition to Johnny, working in the office at the moment. I ask, "What have you said about Grace to the people working in your office?"

"I've told them Grace has gone away to visit a friend and so won't be in to the office for a while. Grace has a friend, Alicia Noble, who works in this office. Alicia knows the truth. You can talk to her if you like. But talk to her outside the office, please."

"Of course," I say.

I feel all eyes in the office are on us as Johnny takes Mike and me to his wife's work cubicle. Grace doesn't work with much privacy. Her work area is tidy and simply and thoughtfully appointed. There are two pictures of small children on her desk. The only sour note is some fake flowers in a vase on the window sill.

Mike quietly asks Johnny, "What exactly does your wife do here?"

"Pretty much anything I need help with. She's only here two days a week. She handles some of my correspondence. I have a bookkeeper, and sometimes Grace helps her out. Grace also pays household bills from this desk. I can't let you access her office computer because everything here is firewall-protected. We're fiduciaries to our clients, you see. When we get to my house, I'll give you Grace's personal laptop."

"And we'll need her cellphone number," Mike says. "We might be able to track the location of her phone."

"Mike," I say, "We tried to track the location of her cell phone yesterday from my office. No luck. The phone account is in Grace's name, so we can't obtain her phone records. And, Johnny, I have my assistant continuing to try to track Grace's phone, which he will be able to do if Grace turns it on."

"Johnny," Mike says, "if you were to report to the police that Grace is missing, they could get a warrant for her phone records. The records could be helpful."

Johnny puts his hand on his chest and gasps. "No," he says. "I don't want to go to the police yet. Please. Let's keep this a private matter for now." Mike and I both, with obvious reluctance, nod our heads.

"Also, Johnny," I say. "There may be cameras along the street here. Do you have any in the parking lot?"

"I don't have cameras in the parking lot. I guess I should have. I've already checked with all the businesses, the offices and restaurants near here. No one has cameras. On Friday afternoon, when I realized Grace hadn't come back to the office from her doctor's appointment, I called her doctor's office. They told me she'd never been there. Impulsively, I walked out of the office into the parking lot where I saw my car parked badly, as I'd parked it that morning. Then I crossed the street to two restaurants, Anderson's and Marino's, and told the managers I was worried about my wife. I asked if anyone had seen anything strange that afternoon. They assured me that no one had. On Saturday, I called Jim Mathis. He's a doctor. His office is across the street on the second floor. I asked him if he had seen or heard anything strange."

"I can check with the police department here and see if they know of any cameras in the area," Mike says.

Opening and closing Grace's desk drawers yields nothing of interest. When we leave Grace's work area, I say to Johnny, "Let's go to your house. If you like, we'll follow you in my car."

We drive several miles before Johnny turns into a compound surrounded by high hedges. The setup is something like my mother's, a big main house and a nearby guesthouse. The difference is that Johnny's house is sitting right next to a house that looks exactly like his house, only smaller.

Johnny invites us in. The interior of the house and the furnishings are expensive but not at all Chinese. I think about Johnny having said, "Once Chinese, always Chinese." Not a drop of Chinese here, until Johnny's mother comes in. She has on a Chinese-style dress, teal silk, her dyed black hair neatly arranged.

We four sit in the living room with fourteen maybe fifteen-foot ceilings. The room is so large, I expect to hear an echo when we speak. I first ask where the children are. "In summer school?"

"Summer day camp," Johnny says. "They

think their mother is on a vacation. I know they see how distraught I am. They keep asking me why I'm so upset all the time."

I ask Johnny if he can give me some pictures of Grace. He says he has some ready for me, along with her laptop computer. He tells me a paper with the passcode to her computer is included with the photos. I ask him to tell me a little about his wife's background.

"Grace grew up in San Diego," Johnny says. "Her parents were immigrants. They still live in San Diego. They know Grace is missing. They want to talk to you. Will that be okay?"

"Of course. Give me their number. If you like, let them know I'll call them tomorrow morning," I say.

Johnny says, "Grace and I met at UCLA as college students. I knew the minute I saw her that she was the one. We met during our junior year and married at the end of our senior year. One interesting thing. Grace has a brother, Terry Wong, an attorney in California, not married, who went to China about a year ago. His trip was supposed to be a vacation. Visit the old country, you know. But after he arrived in China, we lost touch with him. We tried everything we could to find him. About six months ago, Grace went to China with a friend of hers to try to find him. She had no luck. But, well, this whole business of dealing with China can be frightening. I mean, who are those people? I can't relate to them. I have a file on Terry I can give you, in case Grace's disappearance might be related to her brother."

Mike says, "That would be great."

Johnny hands Mike a folder of paper and says, "Ever since Terry disappeared, Grace has been speaking on and off with someone at the U.S. State Department. Her notes about those conversations are in the folder. But, you'll see, the notes are skimpy."

"Did she obtain any information from the State Department that could have been helpful to her?" I ask.

"I don't think so," Johnny says. I ask Johnny if he could give me his files on his employees, so I can research them. "No," he says. "Let's wait a bit on that."

I'm not okay with waiting, but what can I do? I say, "Okay. But if I don't make progress in a day or two, you'll have to let me look into them." Johnny nods as if he's okay with that.

I ask Johnny, "Did Grace have close friends we might talk to, in addition to Alicia, of course?"

"Maureen Bracken, the woman who went to China with Grace. Maureen has since moved to Utah."

Suddenly, Johnny's mother, who has been sitting quietly, calmly, breaks in, saying, "She run way. She run way." Then she begins yelling at Johnny in Chinese. She repeats the same phrase in Chinese over and over. Then suddenly she stops and is utterly composed once again.

"Is everything okay?" I ask.

"Yes. Yes," Johnny says. "My mother is upset. She can't stand to think that something has happened to Grace. She keeps saying that Grace has run away. Honestly, there's no reason Grace would want to run away. We're a happy family." Then Johnny shoots a hostile look at his mother. He goes on, "However, I should tell you that one reason we're happy is that my mother doesn't live with us. She lives in the smaller house on the property. You must have seen it when you drove in." Johnny's mother glares back at him.

"If it's okay, we'd like to take a look around the house," I say. "Especially the bedroom and the kitchen. I find kitchen drawers often hold interesting information relating to the life of a woman of the house. Does Grace have a special work area in the house, a desk or area where she sits to pay bills or do stuff on her laptop? That kind of thing."

"No. She pays bills and things like that while she's at work in my office. She uses her laptop anywhere she wants in the house."

Then Mike and I rise and begin looking around the house. All we find is neutral household items. In a kitchen drawer I find a shopping list Johnny tells me is in Grace's hand. Grace's clothes closet is completely in order. She owns approximately forty-five pairs of shoes. Good taste in clothes. Good taste in shoes. The master bathroom is enormous. Johnny and Grace each have several of their own medicine cabinets. (Do they still call them medicine cabinets?) In her cabinets, I find no medicine, only expensive cosmetics. Mostly Chanel.

"Before we go, Johnny," I say, "I have a few more questions. Does Grace take any medications?"

"No, nothing. This morning I spoke with Dr. Rowan, Grace's primary care doctor, the one she was supposed to see last Friday. I asked him to speak to you. I begged him to please share with you any medical issues that Grace has. He said he can't do that. But I begged. I told him these are special circumstances."

"We'll do the best we can with Dr. Rowan. Please don't worry about that," I say.

Mike asks, "Does Grace have any hobbies? Golf? That sort of thing."

"She likes to knit," Johnny says. He brings his hands up to rest on his chest. Looking down, he says, "She made this sweater for me." The sweater is a lightweight cotton pullover.

"Oh, she's quite good," I say.

"Yes."

Mike says, "Can you tell us how your parents came to the U.S.? When they immigrated, did they come right to Melton?"

"Yes. They did. My father was a physician and a government official in China. He took his medical training in London. The experience made him slightly Westernized, I guess you'd say. Once he was back again in China, he fell out with the Communist Party. He had a friend, Dr. Michael Schiff, who lived in Melton – still does. My father and Dr. Schiff met when Schiff was visiting China. Some doctors' conference. Dr. Schiff sponsored my parents to come to America, specifically to Melton. My parents felt fortunate that there was, and still is, a large Chinese American community in Melton. My father practiced medicine here. I was eighteen when he died."

We all shake hands. Johnny bows. A little. "Oh, the bow is in the DNA," he says, laughing.

On the trip back to Sutterton, Mike tells me that he knows what Johnny's mother was yelling about. "Oh," I say. "You understand Chinese?"

"I do," he says. "Well, I do a little. I went to Purdue for two years. Ahhh, you didn't know that. Yes! And I studied Mandarin, among other things, for the entire two years."

"You didn't!"

"I did."

"Wow. You never told me you went to college."

"I didn't finish, so what's the point of claiming an *alma mater* that I walked out on?"

"Why didn't you finish?"

"I wasn't such a good student. It was a struggle."

I shake my head. "You're crazy," I say. "You know Mandarin, for heaven's sake."

"Yeah. I do."

"You understood what Johnny's mother was yelling?"

"Yes. I think she was saying, 'Tell them about

the other one. Tell them about the other one.' I think that's what she was saying. I think. I haven't spoken or had any contact with Chinese in a long time."

"Okay, so you're telling me what you think she said. You think she said something like, 'tell them about the other one,' possibly meaning 'the other friend'?"

"Yup, that's what I'm thinking."

"So Grace has a friend Johnny doesn't want to tell us about. Hmmm."

The miles pass slowly. Mike falls asleep again. This time I push his arm. "Wake up, dammit!"

"Why?" he says, looking around, dazed. He scratches his head of thick black hair, casually, and he looks out over endless tended fields of green. "So why didn't you go to college, Jan?"

"I did go. Like you, only two years. Vincennes," I say.

"I got a lot out of college," Mike says. "I can't believe we never talked about this before. Now I think I should have hung in there for a B.A. or a B.S. Even though I was kind of a dunce."

"I'm glad I didn't finish. I only went because I knew I wanted to be a cop, and I thought two years of college would give me a little advantage with that," I say.

"Not all forces require two years of college," Mike says.

"Many do," I say. "State police sometimes do. Not Indiana, however. Sutterton doesn't require any college. Which I guess is the reason I didn't assume you went to college."

"College was good for me because it taught me to read books. I mean not only read them, but want to read them."

"What do you read?"

"Right now. Malcolm Gladwell. Do you know him? He's written recently about cops."

"I'm reading Balzac," I say. "Novelist. French guy. I basically read what my dad told me to read."

"Balzac?"

"His works are classics."

"Really? Well, I haven't heard of him."

"Ooooooh," I say, in a snotty tone. "College Boy hasn't heard of Balzac."

He frowns. "Don't call me College Boy. Don't do it. Or I'll have to call you Betty Co-ed."

Mike wants me to come home with him for the night, but I won't because I have to be home for dinner. I drop Mike at his house and go home.

Things are beginning to get crazy. My mother has invited her boyfriend to come to dinner. This is her first boyfriend since Dad died. And this will be the first time I'm meeting him. His name is Jim Peterson, and she refers to him as her "beau," which makes me want to throw up. My mother is not a bad cook, but she's not as good as she thinks she is. Tonight, it's her meatloaf, which I detest. But when you're a grown woman and your mother is still willing to cook for you, you can't be choosy. My mother, though old, dresses like a young woman, mostly in skinny jeans. No grandma calico dresses for her. And I have to admit, she looks good.

Jim shows up late. Eight o'clock instead of seven. So the meatloaf is a little off. Cold, actually, but the potatoes are good. I praise the potatoes. And my mother says, "I know you don't like meatloaf, Jan, but Jim loves it." My mother and I are each sitting at opposite ends of the dining room table. Jim is between us, shifting his attention left to me and then right to her. I believe he is trying to be sincere, ingratiating, but he seems to me to be an oaf. As I'm poking at the meatloaf with my fork, trying to look like I'm eating it, I think "oaf" is the right word. Oaf. That is to say, a large man, not particularly fat, but large, with a lot of gray hair, wearing a cheap suit. I'm thinking, oh, Mother, the suit is too much.

Jim turns his head left to me and says, "Your mother tells me you used to be a policeman."

"Yes," I say. "Yes. Yes. I was."

Jim says, "That must have been interesting."

"Yes," I say. "Yes. Yes. It was. And what do you do, Jim? Mom hasn't told me much about you. Except that she likes you a lot."

Jim lifts his napkin and wipes his mouth, then sits up proudly. He says, "I'm a hay man. Grow it. Sell it. Always have."

"That must be interesting."

"Well, I'm sure it's not as interesting as being a policeman." Then Jim laughs what people who know him surely always describe as Big Jim's hearty laugh. Full of good intention. Full of good feeling. I wonder if my mother is having sex with Jim

Peterson. Probably not. I mean who would have sex with someone who is referred to as a "beau"?

My mother says, "Jim and I met at church, Jan. You could have met him a long time ago if you'd come to church with me."

Then I say, "Hint. Hint. Jim, I think Mom is a little worried about my spiritual life."

Jim says, seriously, "Well, she hasn't said so. I mean not to me."

Later I tell my mom that Jim seems like a nice person. Secretly, of course, I'm hoping she won't marry him and allow him to live with her and me. Would she do that? Let him live here. I mean the house is fabulous. He might want to live here.

CHAPTER 3

I'm up with the sun, then running with my dogs. At first, they yip and jump, happy to be free. Indiana is so full of back roads that are easy to run on. I try to take the dogs to a different road every morning. The sun warms the cool air as we go along. We pass a set of four cyclists, who salute me. I salute them back. Then it's a shower and a walk to the office. I'm going to call Grace's parents, but it's a little early for that, as they're in California. Tom arrives late. I'm thinking, why are men always late? I say nothing about this to Tom. I love Tom. He hands me my favorite Starbucks and asks me what's going on.

I tell him I have Grace Cheung's laptop. I want him to get into it and look around. I'm beginning to trust Tom. Although it's true that I want him to be able to obtain more information during initial contact with prospective clients, I'm coming to realize that he can do more than answer phones and run computer searches. I say, "You can start by calling Johnny Cheung and asking him for Grace's computer password. It was supposed to be included in a file folder of photos he gave me yesterday. But it's not there."

"I'm on it," Tom says.

"Also," I say, "I want you to go online and find as many of Johnny's employees as you can. Do whatever research you can on them. No telephone queries. Stick with the web or the net or whatever it's called. Johnny isn't willing to give me his employee files right now, but eventually he'll have to. Meanwhile, do the best you can."

I'm looking through the file on Terry Wong. It contains information about Grace's trip to China. Nothing very helpful. Mostly receipts for meals and hotels. The file also contains notes Grace kept about her interactions with the U.S. State Department, but the notes contain little of substance. They indicate that right after her brother's disappearance in China, Grace started calling a man named Harvey Lipton at the State Department offices in Chicago. The file contains Grace's hand-written notes of the date and time of each conversation she's had with Lipton, and they indicate that she's called him at the beginning of each month. She's noted that each time she's called she's asked if the State Department has information about her brother. She's also noted after each call: "H. Lipton says no information. But he will look into it." There are two further notes: one states that Grace has an appointment to meet with Lipton on a particular date (before her trip to China), and the other that she and Maureen Bracken are to meet with Lipton (after her return from China) for a "debrief." There are no further notes about the debrief or anything else.

I have Harvey Lipton's office number. I call

him and tell his assistant I wish to speak with him. She wants to know why. I tell her I'm calling about Terry Wong. This information gets me through to Mr. Lipton. I introduce myself as an investigator working for Terry Wong's sister's family. I tell him she's currently missing, and the family is wondering if her disappearance might be related to her brother's disappearance in China.

"She's disappeared?" he says. There's a pause.

I try to be a little reassuring. I say, "She hasn't been gone long, a few days. It may be nothing, a domestic squabble. Something like that. But, as I say, the family's asked me to look into it."

"Oh, I see," Lipton says. "Are you anywhere near my office? Could you come in to talk."

I tell him I'm two hours away and I can be there whenever he wants. "This afternoon? Say two o'clock?"

"Yes," I say.

I spend some time looking closely at the photos of Grace that Johnny has given me. Grace has a sweet smile – as opposed to, say, assertive or joyous – and looks much younger than she is. She has a way of throwing her head back and a little to the side when someone is taking her picture. Large eyes. Straight dark brown hair, highlighted a little, parted on the side, shoulder length. Very hip. Expensive clothes. Expensive suits, jackets. In one picture taken in a park with her kids, even her short shorts have that Gucci look. (Well, I'm not sure what that Gucci look is, but you know what I mean.)

Expensive fabrics. Gold rings on her fingers. A gold Rolex watch with a diamond bezel. Good grief, I think, she might have been abducted for her watch alone! Grace doesn't appear to be unhappy, but in some pics she displays a distant look. A worried look. No, I think, life isn't all roses for Grace.

Tom calls me from the front room. "Grace's parents are on the line."

"Oh," I say. "They called me before I called them. Okay." I get on the line and introduce myself. Mr. and Mrs. Wong are both on the call. The problem is that they both have strong Chinese accents, and I can hardly understand them. We struggle on for a few minutes. The distress in their voices is unmistakable. After a while, they begin to argue with each other and fall into speaking Chinese. Eventually, I say to them, "Please call Johnny. Please call Johnny."

After I hang up, I tell Tom about the problem with Grace's parents. "Have you called Johnny yet about Grace's computer password?" I ask.

"No," he says. "I was about to."

"Okay, tell him I can't understand anything Grace's parents are saying to me. He'll have to interview them and tell me what they say. Tell him they seem to have things they urgently want to say. But I have no idea what those things might be."

Then, I'm in my car and off to Chicago. First, however, I'm stopping, about halfway there, to have lunch with my friend Leslie, who lives in Dayton. Smallish town. Smaller than Sutterton. I've known

29

Leslie since kindergarten. In kindergarten, she told me that when she grew up she was going to be a ballet dancer. And she danced. She happily danced through childhood and adolescence, even in college for a while. Then she met Doug and married him and had two kids and never danced again. She's lucky that Doug has made a good living for the family. Their house is large, five bedrooms. The property has its own forest. Not too big, but still an actual forest. Leslie has been talking to me about how she wants to go back to dancing, now that both her boys are in college. The problem is that she's become obese. She is definitely obese. We never talk about this. And maybe that's not odd. Maybe my friend wants to claim her body, to own it, as they say. She's certainly entitled to see her body as simply her body and not as a problem. We talk about everything but this.

"Baby!" Leslie exclaims as she opens the door. She wraps me in her arms. She has a German shepherd named Big Dog, who immediately, lovingly, jumps all over me. "Stop it, Big Dog," she says.

"No, I love being loved by Big Dog," I say. I sit down on the living room sofa, call Big Dog over, start pulling on his ears. He likes that. I'm facing a wall displaying a painted portrait of Leslie as she was about the time she married. An exquisite ballerina she was, with large blue eyes and shiny blonde hair, severely pulled back, sleek.

"So what do you think about the Sutterton

mess?" Leslie says.

"What Sutterton mess?" I say.

"Well, half the town is for changing the name and half the town isn't."

"Changing the name?" I'm perplexed. I shake my head.

"Well, California is getting rid of the Sutter name because John Sutter, the Sutter's Mill guy, the gold rush guy, abused indigenous people. Enslaved them. That's what they're saying."

"But our Sutterton isn't named after John Sutter," I say. "It's named after Emile Sutter, who was a good guy, who didn't abuse indigenous people."

"Well, you don't know that for sure, do you? John and Emile could be related. Some DNA research is being done."

"This is the most stupid thing I've ever heard," I say. "All the energy that will go into this fight could be used to do something good. But no, people want to waste their time on this? Really?"

"I hope you like shrimp and avocado. I'm so hungry," Leslie says, as she heads for the kitchen. The only type of clothing she ever wears anymore is what I guess I would call a burnoose. Well, not a burnoose. A burnoose is a cloak. But, let's say, she wears tents for dresses. No more classical ballet with this body. I have such an urge to hold her face and say, "Leslie! Why obese? Why? Why?" But I don't, partly because I know what her childhood was like: bad mother. A great beauty, totally self-absorbed, an alcoholic. Always drove big convertibles. Often crashed them. As children, Leslie and I referred to her mother as "VBA," short for "very bad alcoholic." Leslie knew there was a problem. But she has failed to see a connection between her mother's alcoholism and possible issues she has had as an adult.

I walk into the kitchen. We're going to eat lunch in the kitchen, which is a large, sun-filled room, recently renovated and exclusively sporting various shades of gray. Only gray. Gray marble countertops. Gray tile floors. Gray walls. Gray wood furnishings. When the kitchen was being redone, Leslie assured me that gray was the new thing in decorating. Since the reno was completed, every time I walk into the kitchen all I can think is gray, gray, gray everywhere. So gray. Dreary grey, when I know it's supposed to read as crisp, calm, up-to-date gray.

When Big Dog comes to the table with me, he apparently crosses a line. Leslie takes him by the collar and closes him in a bedroom.

Once we're seated in front of slices of avocado and eight cold shrimp apiece, Leslie says, "So you're going to Chicago to work on a big case, right? Tell me everything."

"Not much to tell. A woman from Melton is missing. She went to China a while ago. I'm going to talk to some guy at the State Department."

"As in the 'U.S. State Department'? Sounds fun."

"It won't be. And the worst part is, the guy I'm

seeing is named 'Harvey.'"

"I love that name," Leslie says, and she tears a shrimp from the shell with her teeth.

"You can't!" I say. "Tell me you don't love it! You mustn't love it! How can we continue to be friends?" We both laugh.

"And Mike. How is he?" she asks.

"Mike is Mike," I say. "Still beautiful. Still a good guy."

"He won't be beautiful forever. You should strike while the iron is hot," Leslie says.

"What? Marry him? My dear, I have learned from experience that I don't choose marriage partners wisely," I say.

"Mike is different from those losers you married before. He's different. You could do worse."

"I have done worse," I say.

"I always wondered why Mike hasn't ever gotten married?" Leslie says.

"Oooh, I never told you. He was almost married. To Belinda Morrow. Do you remember her? She was in high school with us. Short. Way too much shiny blonde hair? Always trying out for cheerleader. Never making it."

"No, I don't remember her."

"Belinda and Mike lived together for a long time. Like six years. He kept wanting to get married, but she was not so keen. Eventually, she left him for a woman. She married her. Belinda and her wife now live in Ohio."

"No! Why didn't you ever tell me that?"

"I don't know. It didn't seem like something Mike would want everybody to know."

"But I'm your best friend."

"That's why I'm telling you now. Sometimes I think he was so hurt that he got two boa constrictors to keep women away."

"They don't keep you away."

"They almost do. I keep telling him and telling him that they're bad news."

Leslie pours me a glass of wine, pinot grigio, Santa Margarita, which I love. As she sets down the bottle, she holds up her wine glass as if ready to toast. She says, "Okay, I have tell you something. I'm so into doing something in dance again. I found a place that I think would make a great studio. I want to teach."

I hold my glass up to toast, put it down, then point my fork at her. "I thought we had this conversation. I thought you decided to wait a while. Has something changed?" When, a few weeks ago, we talked about her waiting a while, I assumed she meant she was waiting until after she lost a hundred pounds. Why did I think that? That was crazy of me.

"I'm more serious now than ever. I want so, so much to teach."

"Ballet?" I ask, nodding my head, as if to agree. What am I agreeing with? I don't know.

Finally, the evil, the forbidden words exit my mouth. "Leslie," I say, still pointing that fork. "Your weight."

She's obviously astonished. "My weight?"

she says. "What has my weight got to do with anything?" She's nonchalant, continuing to eat, not looking at me. Then there she is pushing her chair back, placing her hands on the table and staring at me in an extremely hostile manner. "I don't think you've ever wanted me to succeed," she says. "You're always trying to discourage me!"

I've known this woman since kindergarten, and this is our first disagreement. Ever. I'm stunned. "Leslie, I'm sorry," I say. "Of course, I want you to succeed. If you think you're on the right path, please continue. I want you to continue. I mean I don't know anything about ballet. Gee whiz. I have to learn to keep my big mouth shut."

Then her hands are in her lap and her head is in her hands. It's all tears now. "I'm having such a hard time right now. You don't know," she says. "Maybe we should talk about this in a day or two. I know you mean well. I know you love me."

"I do. I do," I say. "Of course. I want you to succeed. I want you to be happy."

"I know you do," she says, sniffing. "I know. We'll talk about this in a few days."

I pull up a chair next to her and we hug. "You're my best friend," she says sweetly, wiping her eyes on the hem of her tent dress. "But you better go. You have to get to Chicago, right?"

"Yes. Yes, I do. Are you okay?" She tells me she's okay. I say, "Can I go say good-bye to Big Dog?"

"Yes. Yes," Leslie says. "Go. Go." She waves me away.

I go into the bedroom where Big Dog is imprisoned. I lie down next to him and hug him. I stay like that for a long time. Big Dog licks my face, then stops, doesn't move. I don't move. I don't want to move. Minutes pass. I know I have to get to Chicago. I know I have to leave this house, but I don't want to. Eventually, Leslie comes into the room. "What are you doing?" she says, sounding genuinely perplexed.

"I don't know," I say. "I don't want to move."

"Okay, darlin'," she says. "You know you can do whatever you want in my house." And she leaves the room. After a few more minutes, I rise. I kiss Big Dog. I grab my purse. I hug Leslie. I leave.

I drive, but my head is spinning. I'm going too fast. I pull onto the interstate and take deep breaths to calm myself. My phone rings. It's Tom.

He tells me he's spoken to Johnny and gotten the password to Grace's laptop. He tells me Johnny has the same problem as I had trying to understand Grace's parents' English. They apparently speak a Chinese dialect that is quite different from Mandarin, so Johnny can't get whatever they're trying to say in either English or Chinese. He can understand some of their English, but not enough for a complex conversation. Tom says, "Mrs. Wong is going to send Johnny something in writing. Chinese. Johnny will be able to understand what it says. Mr. and Mrs. Wong don't use computers. They're sending a letter by Fedex. Did you know written Chinese is one, but spoken Chinese has many dialects, each one sounding as different from every other one as do completely different languages? So two Chinese people, for example, might not be able to speak to each other, but they can communicate with each other in writing."

I tell him I didn't know that. I ask Tom if he's found anything on Grace's computer. He tells me he's just gotten into it.

"One thing I forgot to ask you to do," I say. "Get Maureen Bracken's phone number from Johnny. She's a friend of Grace's. I think she's living in Utah. Find her. But more particularly, confirm to me that she's okay."

"Yes, Boss," he says.

"No. No. No! Don't call me 'Boss.' It's got to be 'Jan.' Okay?"

"Oh," he says. "I thought 'Boss' might be appropriately subservient."

Oh, my God, I'm thinking, he's serious! "No, Tom," I plead. "Please don't think about being 'appropriately subservient.' Don't go there in your brain. Do not!"

"Okay, if you say so," he says. He pauses, then trudges on. "I haven't done the computer research on Johnny's employees yet. Also Mrs. Trumpf called. She needs a stakeout tonight on her husband. She's absolutely certain he's leaving work to meet his girlfriend tonight."

"Alleged girlfriend," I say. "Lannie Trumpf will be the death of me."

"I hope not," Tom says. He says it seriously, as

if he's concerned. I thank him and tell him to text me any new information about Lannie Trumpf's husband's alleged affair. Lannie pays big, so she's entitled to my attention on a few hours' notice, even though my attempts to catch her husband being unfaithful have, so far, over the past two years, yielded nothing. If you're curious about the name 'Trumpf,' then I'll tell you it is the same as Donald Trump's family name was originally. Out of pride for his immigrant ancestors from Germany, Lannie's husband refuses to take the "f' off the end. So "Trumpf" it is. But Lannie and her husband pronounce it "Trump." Go figure.

I call Mike. He's upset that I haven't yet asked Johnny about what his mother said in Mandarin yesterday during the interview. "You haven't asked him about that yet? What the hell! It's important. What's wrong with you?"

"Nothing is wrong with me. Hold your horses," I say. In my mind I can envision him at work in the police station. I know he's pacing. He's a pacer. Three steps this way, turn and three steps back. "Maybe you should be the one to call Johnny and ask him about that?"

"Okay, I will," he says. "But it'll have to be a little later. I caught a case."

"Okay," I say. "Not a problem."

"Also," he says, "I spoke to Dan Tiernan. You know, Melton cop. There are city or county cameras on the street where Johnny's business is, but they haven't been serviced since the 2008 financial crisis.

They don't work."

"Well, that's disappointing."

"You said it. I have to go. Tony and I are on our way out the door. I caught a case."

"Okay, you said that before. Good luck."

CHAPTER 4

It's easy to find the State Department offices in Chicago, but not so easy to find a parking place. I'm late. Once I'm past security, I find that Harvey Lipton has an assistant who behaves more like a bodyguard. She's a slight, blonde young woman who has obviously been given the task of protecting Lipton from all threats, domestic and foreign. She rises from her seat and, although she knows I have an appointment, says, "I'll see if he'll see you." Most forbidding.

She opens the door to what I assume is his office and closes the door behind her. After a brief interlude, she re-emerges and says that she will take me in now. She does. I wonder if this aura of skulkiness and suspicion is something one finds throughout the State Department or is it only the Chicago office that gets its kicks this way.

Before he can say a word, I say to Lipton, "You have a great guard dog out there."

He ignores my statement, holds out his hand across his desk and says, "Call me Harvey. Nice to meet you." I sit, though he doesn't ask me to. We're looking at each other over his desk in a big corner office with many windows. The windows and all the light they let in should make the office feel like a pleasant space to occupy. There is something Lipton's presence adds to the space that kills the possibility of pleasantness. It feels like dead space. Harvey is probably in his fifties. Looks like he's come to a place in his career where he doesn't care that much. About anything.

"Harvey, as I told you on the phone, Terry Wong's sister is missing. I read her notes of conversations she's had with you, both before and after she went to China."

"Oh? What do her notes reveal?"

"That you knew what happened to her brother, but that you wouldn't give her this information or help in finding him."

"I don't believe you."

"Why not? I do have the notes." I think to myself, why am I lying about what the notes say? I lied to a government official, and I don't know why, and he's called me on it. Bummer.

Lipton continues, "I don't believe you because I did tell her what happened to her brother. I told her not to go to China, that it would be a complete waste of time. I told her she wouldn't find him, and she didn't find him."

"What did you tell her happened to her brother?"

"Look. It's simple. China has an authoritarian government. Some people say it's an oligarchy. Certainly, a kleptocracy. I think it's authoritarian. Any authoritarian government spawns dissidents and dissident groups. We know that Terry was involved in a dissident group that was operating in the U.S. The group thought they were operating here secretly. However, the State Department and the FBI knew about the group. We knew that if Terry went to China he would be arrested. We told him so. He went anyway. He's in prison."

"Why did he go?"

"We don't know that. We only know he went. Stupid."

"Where is he in prison?"

"The Chinese don't tell anyone 'where' someone is. Eventually, we'll find out through our agents. But right now, we don't know where."

"Do you think it's possible that Grace upset someone or maybe a bunch of people in China when she was digging around for information about Terry?"

"It is possible. When she returned from China, she gave me a list of the people she had contacted there. We vetted everyone on the list. Some of them were somewhat dangerous people who might go blabbing to a government official about an American woman looking for information on her dissident brother. Yeah. It's possible. That's all I can tell you. Possible."

"And Maureen Bracken, the woman she went to China with?"

"Maureen was completely overwhelmed by the Chinese. Grace could talk to them. She speaks Mandarin as well as her parents' dialect.

Maureen couldn't speak or understand Chinese. She accompanied Grace to meetings, but she had no idea what was being discussed. Is Maureen okay?"

"I don't know. I have someone working on that. She moved to Utah a while ago."

"I would appreciate it if you would let me know if Maureen is okay. Not that I couldn't find out myself."

"I will let you know about Maureen. But tell me something. Simply on the basis of your experience in the State Department and on the basis of what you know about China, what does your gut tell you about whether or not the Chinese might have abducted Grace five days ago?"

Lipton rubs his beard, which is short, nicely trimmed, his only attractive feature, actually. He looks around, then back at me and says, "My gut tells me they didn't. I think if they'd wanted to do something to her, they'd have done it while she was in China. I'm sure they knew every move she made while she was there. It would have been easy to grab her and send her off to the same fate they'd sent her brother to."

We talk a little more about Terry's dissident group. Harvey goes into a long explanation of surveilling techniques, which imparts absolutely nothing of interest. Yet on he drones.

When he's finished, I say, "Thank you for talking to me. I'll let you know about Maureen." Lipton looks relieved. Now he can go back to shuffling papers. As I move toward the door, I turn back and say, "Tell me, why couldn't we simply have had this conversation over the phone? Why did I have to drive all this way for a face-to-face?"

Lipton frowns and says, "This is the U.S. State Department, missy. Get over it."

Then it's out past the guard dog, who scowls at me. I feel a childish desire to bark at her.

After I leave the parking lot, I telephone Johnny. I tell him everything that Lipton has told me. Then I ask him if Grace had told him before she went to China that she knew Terry was in a Chinese prison. And did she tell Johnny that the State Department strongly urged her not to go.

"No," Johnny says. "I never knew any of that. I wouldn't have let her go to China if I'd known any of that."

I tell him, "I guess the good news is that the State Department thinks it's extremely unlikely that the Chinese would abduct Grace in the U.S. We'll close off that line of inquiry for now. I'm coming to Melton tomorrow to talk to the people in the businesses around your office. I know you've spoken to some business owners there, but you were upset. You might have missed something. I have my assistant right now searching for Maureen. Mike is supposed to call you with some questions. Did Mike call you?"

"Not yet," Johnny says. He sounds calm, not at all the intense, worrying Johnny I saw yesterday. "I think I'm going to tell my employees about the situation with Grace."

I tell him I think that's a good idea. I tell him I'll call him in the morning.

CHAPTER 5

Several hours later, at about five o'clock, I drive into the parking lot of the Johnson Reston Company in Sutterton. I sit in my car for a long time waiting for Edgar Trumpf to leave his office. He does so at approximately six fifteen. I've never met Edgar, but I've certainly looked at him intensely on a few occasions over the last two years, while trying to nail him for infidelity to his wife. He's fifty-five-ish, not bad-looking, not fat, which is something of a miracle if you're a man his age and you live in this part of the country. Walks fast, giving the impression of having too much energy. I follow him as he drives in his Mercedes S Class to Westerley's Restaurant, which is a restaurant I love. After he enters the restaurant, I enter the restaurant. He meets two guys at an otherwise empty bar. I don't know the men he's meeting. The three of them order Scotch and start talking about sports. College football. I have no interest in football, so I don't bother to pay attention to what they're saying. I take a seat at a booth in the bar area.

Once I see Edgar and his friends looking at the menu and realize they're planning to eat dinner at the bar, I quietly order a meal that is my favorite at Westerley's: lamb chops with creamed spinach. A salad first, of course. And iced tea. After I order my food, the waitress asks me why I'm whispering.

"I simply have to," I say. "You don't mind, do you?"

"No," she whispers to me. "That's fine." We are now fellow conspirators.

I quietly telephone Tom and ask him to please come meet me here. "But you're on a stakeout, right? Aren't you afraid I'll give you away?" he asks.

"No, Tom," I say. "The guy I'm staking out is engrossed in a discussion of sports. He'll never look my way." I start wondering, how can it be that men have so much to say to each other about football? I don't get it. I believe my perception of football is the perception of most women. That is to say, the game consists of opposing lines of extremely large men, crouched down. Next there's a pile up of these men. Then the lines again. Then the pile up. This goes on for a fairly long time until one man breaks away and runs like hell with his arm enclosing a ball shaped something like an ellipse, as if he were a medieval knight whisking away an infant heir to the throne. Also there is a lot of blowing of a whistle and a lot of waving of hands overhead by a man in a billed cap. To me, that's all there is to football.

It occurs to me as a kind of "eureka" moment that there isn't anything other than sports that American men can talk about with each other. If they talk about anything besides sports, people will think they're gay. They, themselves, will think they're gay. Heaven forfend! What a culture we live in. I once met a man from Belgium who was living in Chicago. He told me that he was at a Chicago party once, and he happened to comment on the exceptionally fine antique furniture in the room of the mansion in which the party was taking place. The pure American to whom he made his comments said, "I don't know anything about furniture, and I certainly don't want to." Then he moved away from the Belgian, as if to shun him. How dare a man in America speak to another man in America about anything but sports! (Maybe sometimes they can talk about women. Or possibly their children. But only if the children get into the University of Michigan Law School or are so successful that they can retire at age 48.)

After I'm finished with my salad and half-way through the lambchops, Tom arrives. He skulks in, hiding his face as he sidles up to my booth. "Should we whisper?" he asks.

"Yeah, a little," I say. "You want anything to eat?"

"I would love some pie and coffee." I order him pie and coffee. There's a bit of confusion over the pie. It's a berry pie. Tom wants to know what the berries are.

"What difference does it make, what berries?" I whisper.

"Okay," he whispers. "Berry pie then." He waits a while and then says, "How did things go with the State Department?"

"There's nothing to the China connection. At least that's what the State Department believes. So we're going in other directions now."

"Okay," Tom says, "I've done what research I can on people I found online in Johnny's office."

"When I see Johnny tomorrow," I say, "I'll have him send you his office files on all his employees."

"Good idea," Tom says. "Every employee I could identify online is okay, except for one secretary who has a fifteen-year-old DUI. You'll be happy to know I've found Maureen Bracken and she's okay. I spoke to her. She's gotten married. She's taken her husband's last name. She's going to have a baby in three months. I didn't grill her about Grace. I think you should do that."

"Yes, I'll do that. I'm relieved to hear she's okay," I say.

"As for Grace's computer, I got into her gmail account. I studied it. She deletes a lot."

"How do you know that?"

"Because there's not much in the way of emails available. She assiduously cleans out her emails. Johnny says his business has a Facebook account, but he says neither he nor Grace has a personal Facebook account. No other social media."

"Why not?"

"I asked him why not. He said he and Grace have invasion of privacy concerns with some social media sites. They're not the only ones in this country to have such concerns, as you know."

"In her gmail account, everything is totally normal. She's looked at a lot of gardening websites. She looks for special kinds of wool knitting material. 'Yarn' I guess it's called. Everything in her gmail is kind of boring. I was hoping for something racy to brighten up my day, but no go."

"You don't know what 'yarn' is?"

"Well, now I do."

"Who does she email with?"

"Nobody. Maureen Bracken. Alicia Noble. You told me Alicia is one of Grace's friends. That's pretty much it. She gets lots of emails from department stores. Bloomingdale's. Saks. She orders expensive clothing. And handbags. She loves handbags."

"The emails with her friends, what are they about?"

"They're about meeting for lunch. That's Alicia. With Maureen, it mostly has to do with Maureen's life, which I gather has been quite interesting since she moved to Utah. You know, marriage, baby coming. There's not much about Grace's life. I have the feeling Grace and Maureen talk to each other a lot on the phone."

I thank Tom for his good work and tell him I want him to run with the dogs in the morning. I'm beat and I'm going to sleep in. I can tell he's not too excited about this because it means he has to take the dogs from my mother's house and put them in the office for the night. He doesn't like to deal with my mother. He's not alone in that respect.

After Tom leaves, I sit and sit. I order dessert,

a chocolate brownie with ice cream. I pay the bill and sit. Isn't Edgar ever going to leave? I think, c'mon, Edgar, let's go! Along about nine o'clock, he finally rises, leaves his friends behind. I follow him out. I get in my car and follow his S Class. I watch him drive to his impressive home in the prestigious Westgate development. He drives into the garage, closes the garage door. Edgar is a good boy. I have earned a lot of money this evening, and Edgar is home free. Win. Win.

Once home and in bed, I have a hard time sleeping. Grace is on my mind. And my friend Leslie is on my mind. Grace, where are you? Where have you gone? And Leslie, how can I mend our rift? And I think there is a rift, although she acted as though there weren't. I think about the enormous country of China and how little I know about it.

I remember a story my dad once told me about Mao Zedong. After Mao died, his personal physician wrote a book about him. In the book, the physician tells of once, late in Mao's life, being summoned by Mao. Mao told him that he had decided he wanted never to die. He told his physician that he expected him to come up with a way to ensure his immortality. The physician agreed that he would get right on it. I remember my father chuckling as he told this story. I was eleven or twelve at the time. I asked if Mao's craziness about living forever had something to do with the fact that he was Chinese. My dad said, "No, this is the craziness of the autocrat, a dictator."

"What do you mean?" I asked.

He explained. "A dictator is a person who is isolated, has no friends, has no peers, no one who loves him. Isolation is bad for the mind. Mao, isolated as he was, lost it. He decided he would arrange things so he would never die. But it turned out that one of the few things he couldn't bring about was his own immortality." Then he added something like: "Always remember that it takes courage to accept our mortality, to live knowing someday your life will end. Autocrats have no courage about mortality or anything else. Remember that."

CHAPTER 6

The next morning, I'm up late. Mom makes me breakfast, scrambled eggs with tiny bits of sauteed onion mixed in, fresh-squeezed orange juice. I'm still in my bathrobe and bunny slippers. (I do love my bunny slippers.) I'm sitting at the kitchen table, shoveling in the scrambies. My mother seems sad, warming her hands on a mug of coffee. "Mom," I say. "What's up? Something's wrong. What is it?"

My mother is nothing if not coy. "It's nothing, dear," she lies. She has rollers in her hair, like rollers from the year 1970. She still wears her hair as if it were 1970. Rolled and a little teased. Colored, of course. A lot of hair spray to insure a solid wind-proof formation. What used to be dark brown hair is now light brown hair with golden tips. "Well," she adds. "If you must know, it's Jim."

"Already?" I say. "I just met him night before last. Already something has gone wrong?"

"I met his daughters yesterday, and later he told me they don't like me. They don't think I'm right for him."

"How could you not be right for him? Did they say?"

"They think I'm 'too, too'."

" 'Too, too'? What does that mean?"

"I don't know."

"Mom, this is crazy," I say. As with Leslie, I'm pointing a fork at her, jabbing the air to make my point. "His daughters are grown people. What has their liking you or not liking you got to do with anything? This man is a baby!"

"Don't say that," she says. "He's a nice person."

"Oh, Ma, he's an oaf!"

"An oaf!" she repeats. Her back is up now. "An oaf! You who married first a child molester and then a convicted felon, you think you have the right to judge my choice of a man?"

My fork goes down. My hands go to my lap. I am trounced by the truth. "Ma, you are a beautiful and most unusually interesting woman," I say, exaggerating a little. "I think Jim is not for you if, as you say, he's a man who will allow his grown children – who after all have lives of their own now – to have the last word about his choice of girlfriend. That's all I'm saying, Mom."

Then she starts to sob. I go to the counter, grab some tissues and bring them back to her. That's two women in two days whom I have brought to tears. You're doing great, Jan.

"Okay, dear," she says. "I understand what you're saying. Frankly, this was a huge shock to me. When he said what he said, I could hardly believe it. He's a good Christian man, no doubt about it. I like him so much." Her sniffles are drying now. She adds, "I'm sorry I said those things about your husbands, even if it was the truth."

"Yes, Ma, it was the truth. Although in fairness, husband number one was not a child molester when I married him, and husband number two was not a felon when I married him."

"Yes, I know, dear," she says, still with the sniffles.

Once I'm dressed and in my office, I telephone Mom to make sure she's okay, even though she's only about two hundred feet from where I'm sitting. She tells me that Jim has telephoned her. They've made a date to talk. I tell her I think that's great. I don't think that's great. He's an oaf and a stupid oaf, at that.

But now I have other things to deal with. I have to speak with Maureen and with Alicia Noble. I have to speak with Johnny. I have to speak with Mike. My head is reeling. And, wouldn't you know it, Lannie Trumpf walks in!

I can hear her pushing past Tom and on toward my office in her clickety clicking stiletto heels. She throws her purse, which is large and has hard sides, onto my desk, and sits. She quietly stares at me for a while. She is in her late forties and, though her eyebrows are a little too darkly penciled, still a beautiful woman. But I have to say that when she silently stares at me she's as scary as a mad warthog. She pulls a cigarette case from her purse. Takes a cigarette, lights it with a match and then looks around, as if she's dumbfounded that there is no ashtray easily available into which she can deposit the dead match. Finally, she drops the match on the floor. I pick up the telephone and call Tom in the other room. "Tom," I say, calmly. "Please bring an ashtray into my office for Mrs. Trumpf."

"We don't have any ashtrays," Tom says.

"Bring something," I say. He brings in a saucer.

Lannie Trumpf says, "Well?" This "well" is fully loaded.

"I have nothing inappropriate to report," I say.

"What do you mean" Lannie says.

"Your husband left work last night at six fifteen. I followed him to Westerley's Restaurant, where he met two other men. They ate dinner at the bar, while carrying on a long, boring conversation about college football. Then I followed your husband home, where, as you probably know, he arrived a little after nine o'clock."

"That was it?" Lannie is upset, clearly, but I'm not sure why.

"That was it," I say.

Sternly, she says, "I'm telling you I know he is doing this, and I will catch him!" Then she puts out her cigarette in the saucer and leaves. As she goes into the front room, Tom (God bless his courageous little heart!) asks Lannie if she would like to pay her bill now. She says, "Yes," and from what I hear after that, I conclude that she does pay.

I call Mike and ask him if he spoke with Johnny yesterday about what Johnny's mother said in Mandarin during our interview. He tells me Johnny told him his mother's remarks meant nothing, that she was confused about the names of Grace's friends. "Do you believe him?" I ask Mike.

"Nope," he says. "But, regardless of whether or not Johnny is lying, I have more thoughts about this case. Let's have dinner tonight. My place. I'll get Italian take-out. Seven-ish?"

"Okay," I say. "But only if Curly and Stretch are in their cages when I arrive. Otherwise, if I have to go looking for them, I won't come in." I tell him I'm planning to drive to Melton in a few minutes.

"Oh, wait," Mike says. "I forgot something. Tell Johnny I know someone who can get Grace's cell phone records, but it'll cost him six thousand dollars."

"Great!" I say.

Then Mike says, "I didn't tell you that." And I agree with him that he didn't tell me that.

Once in the car, I telephone Maureen. I tell her the situation with Grace. I tell her I've spoken to Harvey Lipton at the State Department. I ask her if there's anything she can tell me that would help us find Grace. "Anything about your trip to China; anything about the State Department; anything that came up in your friendship generally," I say.

She tells me that being in China was somewhat disconcerting, that she felt lost a lot of the time because she couldn't understand Chinese. "I felt like I was hanging onto Grace for dear life," she says. "I wouldn't let Grace out of my sight. I knew she was looking for her brother. So we met with a lot of people there, but I had no idea what was going on in those meetings. I will say that I don't think Grace was ever frightened when we were in China. Our hotel was nice, though I thought the food wasn't great. Grace was disappointed in the food, too. She's an upbeat kind of person. We had fun while we were there. We laughed a lot. She did tell me she liked being away from her family. She felt she needed some time away, but I don't know why she felt that way."

I tell Maureen I understand that after the trip to China she was with Grace for the State Department debriefing with Harvey Lipton, and she says she was. "I did feel a little fear when we were talking to the State Department guy. He spoke about the Chinese in an almost paranoid way, I would say. He tried to frighten us. I thought, why would he talk this way after we've been there and returned safely? Could the Chinese hurt us in America? I asked him point blank about that. He said he thought not. And I thought, if that's the case, why are you trying to scare us? I don't know. I was happy to get away from the guy. Do you think the Chinese have something to do with Grace's being missing?"

"I tend to think not," I say. "As Lipton said to me, if the Chinese wanted to harm Grace, they would have done so when it was easy to do, while she was in China."

Maureen pauses and says, "Grace is missing. That's frightening. What are the police saying about this?"

"Johnny won't tell the police about this. He says it's a Chinese thing not to deal with the police. Did you know this?"

"No," Maureen says. "But I do know from my friendship with Grace that the Chinese Americans tend to circle the wagons when any of them feels at all threatened."

I thank Maureen for her time and ask her to call me or email me if anything more comes to mind. She stops me from hanging up, saying, "I should have told you this at the beginning of our conversation, but I didn't feel comfortable doing so. Here's the thing: I don't think Grace's marriage is the happiest. I think it's okay, but not great. I don't know how it isn't great. She wouldn't tell me. But she gets depressed. Not in China, but here in her day-to-day life. She's Chinese American so she keeps a lot inside. You can't pry it out of her."

After I hang up, I drive along and think, well, now I have two pieces of real information. First, the Cheung marriage is not great, and, second, Grace has periods of depression. I call Harvey Lipton at the State Department to tell him that I've located Maureen and that she is thriving. He says he's grateful for my call.

I then call Johnny to tell him I'm on my way to Melton. I know there's a coffee shop near his office. I tell him that after I finish checking the businesses and offices in the area, I want to meet with Alicia at this coffee shop and then I want to meet there with him. He agrees. I tell him to bring six thousand dollars in cash to our meeting. He says he will. I wait for him to ask me what the money is for. He doesn't ask.

It's a beautiful day in Melton, and I can easily park right downtown.

I start with two nearby doctors' offices near Johnny's building. Visits to these offices yield nothing. I speak to everyone in both offices: the doctors, the receptionists, the nurses. No one saw or heard anything last Friday when Grace disappeared. Then I visit two pharmacies and an antique shop. Again nothing. I visit the two restaurants that Johnny ran to last Friday. Oddly, everyone in the restaurants is uncooperative, as if threatened in some way. I apologize. I give my card to everyone I speak to, asking them to call me if anything at all occurs to them, something they saw or heard that didn't seem right.

I hit a bit of pay dirt at the third restaurant I visit. It's also across from Johnny's building, but a bit east. After talking with a few people in the restaurant, I decide to sit and have lunch. I order a burger, fries and a beer, and start chatting with my waitress, a young woman probably in her early twenties, who has a kind of sweetness and innocence about her, dressed as she is in her big red-and-white-checked regulation skirt, as is worn by all the women working in the place. I tell her who I am and ask her if she's heard anything about the disappearance. Has she heard anyone say anything about it?

"Well, I saw something," she says. Her eyes widen. "It was strange. About the time they say Mrs. Cheung left her office, there was this big red car, noisy car, I mean very noisy car, that literally squealed out of the parking lot by Mr. Cheung's building. I saw this. I thought it was kind of strange. I mean Mr. Cheung's office has mostly financial people working in it. Accountants, people like that, right? Why would somebody driving that kind of car be in that parking lot? That's what I thought. Of course, I could be wrong. It's possible it was a rock star or someone like that going to see his accountant. But we don't have rock stars around here, except for Jimmy Dillon."

"Jimmy Dillon?" I say.

"Yeah, he's the only real rock star around here."

"I haven't heard of him," I say.

"He's big," she says. "He lives in Delphi."

"Oh," I say.

I ask her if she knows the make of the car she saw, and she says no. "Anything else you can tell me?" I say.

"No," she says. "That's all I know. And it might not even be related to Mrs. Cheung, you know."

I ask her for her name. She tells me she's Mary Nell Crocker. She gives me her cell phone number. "Okay, Mary Nell," I say. "Thank you so much. Take my card. If you think of something more, call me."

I go to the coffee shop where I told Johnny yesterday I would meet with him and Alicia. I talk to everyone there about Grace, but learn nothing. I sit, order coffee and call Johnny. I ask him to send Alicia to me. Alicia arrives a few minutes later, a tall woman, dark hair piled high, nice-looking, not pretty, wearing a gray business suit with high-heeled shoes. She orders coffee, then sits, shifts a bit in her seat. She has blue eyes that seem to bore right through me. They have a glacial quality, a hard ice quality. She seems frightened. She shakes a packet of sugar and says, "I met Grace at work a few years ago, when she first started coming into the office. We weren't friends to begin with. But then as time went on, we realized we have a lot in common. We're about the same age, have kids, though she's married and I'm divorced. She and I started having lunch. To tell you the truth, that's about it. It's lunch. We don't see each other otherwise. I don't know why. We should. I've always thought Grace was a little stand-offish. I've always thought that may have something to do with the fact that I'm not Chinese."

I say, "Or that she is Chinese?"

"Yeah, something like that. I have to tell you that she is a nice person, a good person, would help you any way she could. But sometimes she gets depressed. She won't admit that she gets depressed. She calls these periods simply her 'sad times.' I can always see this when it happens. I've told her she can do something about this so-called 'sadness,' but she won't listen to me. No head doctors for her. No medication for her. She wants to tough it all out. Sorry, I hope I'm not speaking ill of her."

"You're not speaking ill of her. I've heard about Grace's depression from others. I won't tell Johnny anything you tell me. I know he's your boss. You don't want to get in trouble with the boss."

"Yes," she says. "That's it exactly. I knew before I came here today that I wanted to tell you the real deal on Grace. But, yes, Johnny is my boss, so there's that, too."

"Do you think it's possible that either Grace or Johnny is seeing someone outside the marriage?"

"Oh, I hate to say this, but I do think it's possible."

"Why do you say that?"

"There's some coldness that I see between them in the office. It's that coldness that makes me worry. It started a few months ago. Something might be going on. That's what I keep thinking. You do know that Grace is absolutely gorgeous?"

"Yes, but then, so is Johnny," I say.

"Well, I guess he is. I don't see that aspect of him. He's my boss. He can be demanding. I look at him and see a demanding boss. I'm thinking of leaving the firm, but to get another job as a financial adviser I'd have to uproot my kids and move to Indianapolis or Chicago. So I keep putting it off, because I don't want to move."

"Johnny's demanding?"

"Only as a boss. Never, as far as I can tell, with Grace. There's coldness, but never an unkind word from him to her. And, frankly, most of the coldness is on her part toward him." Then we both sit quietly for a minute or two. I thank Alicia, and she smiles and reaches across the table and takes both my hands in hers. She tells me she hopes she's been able to help me, and I tell her she has. She leaves.

I call Johnny and ask him to meet me. When he arrives, he goes to the counter and puts in a complex coffee order. No simple coffee with cream and sugar for him. A splash of this. A splash of that. Then he joins me. I tell him about my morning and the information Mary Nell has given me about the big, noisy red car. He says, "Well, no one in my office heard that. Some of my people have offices that look right over the parking lot. No one heard that."

I ask Johnny if he got an odd reaction from anyone in his office when he told them about Grace's disappearance.

He says, "No. People seemed a little stunned, but that was it."

"Did anyone say anything to you that might be helpful?"

"No," he says.

I tell him I want him to email me the names of everyone who works in his office. I tell him to include all information he has about each person so I can check backgrounds. He says he will. I ask him if he received a letter today from Grace's parents. He says he has, and he hands it to me. "It's written in Chinese," he says, stating the obvious. "I can tell you what it says. It says that Grace's parents worried about her when she was an adolescent, that she suffered from bouts of what they call 'sadness.' They worry that this may have become a problem for her again. They are worried she may have run away or hurt herself. I think these are the concerns of over-protective parents. I've never seen Grace depressed or sad unless there was a good reason to be sad."

"Do you mind if I take the letter?" I ask.

"Of course not. But why? I mean you can't read it?"

"I can't," I say. "But I may know someone who can. Look, Johnny, I need to look at everything. All of it. Chinese. English. Whatever. All of it. Okay?"

"Yes, of course, okay," he says.

Once again, I urge him to go to the police. He says he won't. I say, "Johnny, you may be worried that the police wouldn't put much time into investigating the disappearance of a Chinese American woman. And you might be right. But you also might be wrong. And anyway, I'll stay on this case regardless of whether or not you bring in the police."

"It's not that," Johnny says. "Of course, I know the police will do nothing to find a missing Chinese American woman. I know this. Our whole Chinese community knows this. My issue with the police is about dealing with the authority they have. They mistreat members of our community. They treat the blacks and the Chinese the same way, as if we're not human beings. I don't want to have anything to do with them."

I say, "Then I can tell you I've found someone who can access Grace's cell phone records. If the police did this with a warrant, it would cost you nothing. But if you want to do this on your own, it will cost you six thousand dollars. That's the cash I asked you to bring. It's up to you. I think it would be helpful to have those records."

"I brought you the money," he says. And he hands me an envelope.

Before I leave, I say, "I have Tom continuing to try to track Grace's phone, which he can do if she turns it on. Johnny, what do you think happened to Grace?"

"I think she's run away," he says. "Not forever. For a while. To clear her head or something."

"Why would she do that?"

"Look," he says. "My wife and I are happy, but she's a bit high strung. She likes to go off by herself once in a while, sometimes with friends, but usually she'll tell me when she's going and where she's going. This time she didn't, but it's not the end of the world. She'll be back. But, well, of course, because she didn't say anything to me last Friday when she disappeared, I have concerns. That's why I hired you. In case, you know. In case, she didn't take off on her own."

"Why didn't you tell me this before, this stuff about her taking off on her own?"

"I don't know. I was upset. I wanted you to find her, no matter what the situation was."

"Is this the first time she may have gone off on her own without telling you?"

"She did this once before. A couple years ago."

"Aha," I say. "And where did she go that time?"

"To Florida. She has a cousin who lives in Palm Beach. I've been calling the cousin every day. She hasn't heard from Grace or seen Grace since last Friday. She shares my concern about where Grace might be. I'll give you information about the cousin, so you can contact her if you want to."

"When she went to see her cousin, did she keep her cell phone turned off?"

"No. Once she got to Florida, she called me to let me know where she was."

"You should have told me this, Johnny. You should have told me all of this," I say.

"Well, now you know," he says.

"One last thing, Johnny," I say. "In some of the pictures of Grace that you gave me she's wearing a lot of jewelry, including a gold Rolex watch. If someone has abducted her, it's possible they understand the watch could be worth forty or fifty thousand dollars. They might try to sell it, pawn it, along with the other jewelry she wears. The Rolex probably has no distinguishing features, but the other jewelry, the rings might be identifiable. Tell me about them."

Johnny says. "I bought that watch as a present for Grace. The back is engraved with the letters 'GWC.' So it's identifiable."

"I don't see how you could engrave the back of a Rolex," I say.

"Well, I had it done. That's what the back of her Rolex says."

"Okay," I say. "That's good to know. And the rings?"

"One ring she wears all the time is an emerald ring. The stone isn't large, and it's not worth much. The other is a plain gold band, her wedding ring that she wears all the time. Also not worth much. Neither has engravings. When we were married, I couldn't afford anything expensive. That's why a few years later I bought a Rolex for Grace. You might be able to find the Rolex if someone has stolen it and sold it."

"Yes. That's great information. Thank you."

On the drive home, I feel somewhat defeated. I can't help thinking it would be good for Johnny to have the resources of the Melton cops to assist in finding Grace. He says he's concerned that the police would do nothing, but maybe he's more concerned that they would do nothing and then one day simply lock him up. Until I know a crime has been committed, there's not much I can do about bringing cops in, except on an informal basis.

There are two pawn shops that I know a little way off the interstate. On impulse, I decide to get off the highway and check them both for Grace's watch. The first one, Delaney's, is closed when I arrive. Then I go to Arnold's, which is always open early and late, and ask about Rolex watches. Arnie shows me a few, but nothing in gold. But then Arnie knows who I am and what I do. He may be hiding something from me. I give him my card and say, "Arnie, my mom is hankering for a gold Rolex. Please call me if one comes to you. I need one for her birthday, and I don't want to pay retail."

"No problem," Arnie says. He has his arms crossed over his chest.

"Be a good boy, Arnie," I say. "Don't hide things. They'll get you in the end."

"What does that mean?" he asks.

"Whatever you want it to mean," I say, and I'm on my way. I like speaking in riddles. Riddles can be scary. They could scare someone into showing me a woman's gold Rolex, but not today.

Back on the road again, I call Tom. He says the office has been quiet today. I don't know whether that's good news or bad news. He says he's still trying to track Grace's phone. No luck. I tell him I'm staying at Mike's tonight so he'll have to run with the dogs in the morning.

CHAPTER 7

I stop first at my mother's house. As I get out of the car, I think of something my father said when, several years ago, I moved back into this house after I split from my second ex. Dad said, "As Clare Booth Luce once said, 'The only good thing about divorce is that you get to sleep with your mother.'" And, yes, here I am, sleeping with my mother. (Not literally.)

I walk in and she's making dinner. It seems a little early for that. My mother tells me Tom called her to say he's picking up the dogs and so she's invited him to dinner. It's that horrible meatloaf again, so I'm happy I'm going to Mike's. "I thought you didn't like Tom?" I say.

"I like company," she says. "I take it where I can get it. Anyway, Tom has grown on me."

"Great," I say, as I give her a hug. "I stopped by to see how you are." I can tell she's had her hair done. Perfect helmet. "How was your conversation with Jim this morning?"

"We met for lunch," she says. I never before took notice of the fact that she's still wearing the set of engagement and wedding rings that my father gave her. I think that's a little odd for someone who is, as she says, "being courted." But who am I to say?

I never had engagement rings or wedding rings. At least not the good ones. I had silver. I would like to have good ones. Gold. Diamonds. I would. Deep down inside I'm a girly girl.

I pick up an apple and bite into it. Terrible. Sour. I throw it away. "Don't do that," my mother says. "I bought those today."

"You should return them. They're terrible," I say. "How did the lunch with Jim go."

Those seem to be magic words. My mother starts waving a wooden spoon around and does a little happy dance. "Very well," she says.

"Tell me everything," I say. "Tell me. Tell me."

"We chit-chatted for a little while, ordered some food. We were at Saxon's. The food there is so good. Have you been there?"

"Of course, Mom. So then what?"

"I told him I wanted to talk a little about his relationships with his daughters. He said he's close to Megan, probably because she's not married yet. To tell you the truth, I don't think Megan will ever get married. But that's okay. She has a great career as a cosmetologist. You know that. His relationship with Astrid is not as close, but she's married and has children and all that."

"Where do these women live, Mom? And exactly how old are they?"

"Megan is thirty. Astrid is thirty-two. They both live in Indianapolis. Jim and I talked and talked, and then something happened."

"What happened, Ma?"

"I told Jim that it seemed strange to me that his grown daughters, who – as you said, Jan – have lives of their own, would interfere with his choice of a girlfriend. Then he slapped my face."

"He what! He slapped you! In the restaurant! How many times?"

"Just the once. Maybe twice." Now she's a little sheepish. "I think he wanted to give me a few little smacks for criticizing his daughters. Not an unreasonable reaction, if you ask me. He was protecting them from criticism."

"Oh, my God, Mom!" I say. Then I sit at the table, elbows on the table, face in my hands. I do have a way of flipping out at times. This is one of those times. "Oh, Mom, there are only two kinds of men in the world. Those who hit women and those who don't. I don't know why, but there is nothing in between. There's no guy who slaps a woman once and doesn't do it again for ten years. There's nothing like that. Men either are hitters or they aren't hitters. Jim is a hitter, Mom. You have to get him out of your life!"

In a disgusted tone of voice, my mother says, "It was two smacks. I don't know why I even told you. I should have known you wouldn't understand. You're a feminist type of person who is down on men because you think they're all criminals. That's what being a policewoman does for you!"

"That's not true, Mom. I'm not down on all men. That's ridiculous. But I ask you, Mom, did Dad ever raise a hand to you in your more than forty years of marriage? No, he did not. Because he was not a hitter. You don't know what it's like to live with a man who's a hitter. It's bad."

"Those little slaps were nothing!" She stands looking away from me, stirring something in a bowl on the countertop. She wipes her hands on her apron and opens the oven and peeks in. Then she turns and says, "I knew you'd make a big deal out of it."

"Okay," I say. "But why did you tell me if you knew I would make a big deal out of it? I think you told me because you wanted me to let you know whether or not it is a big deal. Well, Ma, it is a big deal! I'm letting you know." I raise my hands and start pulling on my hair. Time to leave.

When I get to Mike's, he's busy putting out plates and glasses and opening foil packages of cooked pasta. I tell him about Jim slapping my mother. He stops working and gives me a hug. He says, "Are you actually worried that Jim, the oaf, is a woman-beater?"

And I say, "Well, why wouldn't I be worried? I should be."

"There's nothing you can do about your mother's choice at this point," he says. "Later on, if you think she's in trouble, you can intervene. You know her well. You'll know if something is going on with Jim that isn't right. And I think it's a good sign that she told you about the slaps. It means she's not as sure as she says she is about what they meant. She might think about it for a while, and then agree with you. You never know."

I'm somewhat crestfallen. "But what if he beats her up?"

"He hasn't beaten her up, my dear," he says. "Let's be calm and eat this wonderful dinner I've brought you. We have other things to worry about and discuss."

I think, wonderful dinner? Not so much. Two pastas, two crummy-looking salads and a bottle of Chianti. I feel like being ornery. "I won't sit down until you assure me that Curly and Stretch are in their cages."

"They are," Mike says. "Happily curled up in their cages. Would you like to see them?"

"No." I sit. I eat. I'm grumpy. I don't talk. Until I do. I say, for the nine-hundredth time, "Why snakes, Mike?"

"You've asked me that so many times. Can't you let it go?"

"No, I need to know the absolute truth about the snakes, Mike."

"Well, as I always tell you when you ask me this question, I want to have pets that are not too much work. Curly and Stretch don't bark. I don't have to take them for walks. They're easy. We've been over this before. Many, many times before." He uses his fork to curl linguini into a spoon. He's paying close attention to this process of loading the fork and raising it to his mouth. I find this irritating. I want his attention.

"I told Leslie about you and Belinda."

In a nanosecond, he's angry. "Why would you do that? Why would you tell her about something that was so humiliating to me? Why? Why? I thought you were my friend!"

I explain to him that I want to understand why Belinda's leaving him was so humiliating to him. He yells at me: "Because she left me for a woman!"

"So what?" I yell back. "What difference does it make whether she left you for a man or she left you for a woman or she left you for a sheep dog? Who cares?"

"You don't get it, do you?" Now he's leaning toward me across the table, one arm stretched toward me. "For a man to lose a woman to another man is one thing. But I lost her to a woman, and that is a whole other kettle of fish."

Kettle of fish, I think. Interesting use of the phrase.

He goes on, "I had a chance to convince her that she could be a normal heterosexual woman. But she chose something else. I failed." Now he's digging into his linguini with his fork, looking down at the bowl. "Man, I loved her!"

I'm speaking calmly now: "A woman choosing to be with a woman is not a choice. Surely, you must understand that. Or are you still living in the nineteenth century? Or even the twentieth century?"

"How can it not be a choice?"

"It's not. Being gay is a difficult thing to come

to terms with. In this little town, can you imagine how hard it must be for a child who understands she's gay to accept herself? And what about all the anxiety she feels about the reactions other people will have if she comes out?"

"It's a choice." He's so insistent. This is not like him.

"It isn't. If it were a choice, who would make that choice? No one. At least not in Indiana." He continues to pick at the linguini. "Look at me," I insist. "Look at me. Tell me, did you make a choice to be attracted to women, to have sex with women? Was that ever a choice you made? To forgo men in favor of women?"

"No. Of course not."

"Sexual preference is not a choice."

"Well, I'm sorry, but I think Belinda went off the rails."

"She came to terms with who she is. She did you a favor by leaving. You didn't fail at all. You did not fail, my friend. You did not fail."

"I'm sorry, Jan. I will always feel like I failed."

"But you didn't. You have to get past this. Maybe you could even come to terms with what Curly and Stretch represent to you."

Mike throws up his hands and says, "Oh, no, here comes the Freudian bullshit! You know, Jan, sometimes a cigar is just a cigar!"

And I say, "And sometimes a snake is just a penis. Just sayin'. Sometimes." I throw my arms up, too. Two can play the arms-up game. "And one more thing, while we're at it. There is something misogynistic in you saying it would have been better if she'd left you for another man rather than for a woman."

"You think I'm a woman-hater?"

"A little," I say. "Maybe not a full-blown hater, but certainly you have issues about women."

"Do you want to keep arguing?" he asks. We sit and glare at each other for a long time. He cracks his knuckles, which he knows I hate.

Eventually, I stand. I say, "No, all I want to do is sleep."

The next morning, I wake before Mike does. I tip toe into the shower, then dress quietly and tip toe into the kitchen to clean up the dishes and food from last night. Mike follows right after me into the kitchen. "I want to eat the salad," he says.

"But it's been sitting out all night. It's all wilted and gooey," I say.

"I like wilted and gooey," he says. He picks up a fork and begins to eat a disgusting wilted room temperature salad.

"Guess what I have for you?" I say.

"Don't make me guess. I hate having to guess." What a grump he is this morning.

"I have a letter from Grace's parents."

"Alright!" Ah, not such a grump now!

"And I have six thousand in cash."

"Oh, wow! Cash is king!"

"No," I say. "Cash is queen!" I go into the bedroom and pull from my handbag said letter and the envelope of cash.

After I give these items to Mike, he says, "I will slowly translate this letter. Slowly, because my Chinese is a little rusty. I speak Chinese better than I read it. I'll take the cash to my phone records guy first thing. I'll call you when he has something on Grace's phone."

"Another thing," I say. "Grace was wearing a gold Rolex when she disappeared. It has the initials 'GWC' engraved on the back. We should be looking for it. Pawn shops. How many are there? A lot?"

"You can't engrave the back of a Rolex," Mike says.

"I know. But somehow Johnny did it. On the way back from Melton yesterday, I checked at Arnold's Pawn Shop. No gold Rolexes. If you happen to go past other pawn shops while roaming around today, you might check to see if you can find it. Please call your pal Dan Tiernan in Melton, and ask him to keep his eyes open for the watch."

"Of course," he says. I take his face in my hands. He has a little line of sweat over his lips. I kiss the sweat off and tell him I love him. He says, "No, you don't. Why are you saying that?"

I say, "Because I love you. As they say in the trade, 'you're one of the good guys.'"

"What trade?" he says. I don't answer. He says again, "What trade?" And then I'm out of there

CHAPTER 8

As I pull my car up to the front of the guesthouse-slash-office, I notice Edgar Trumpf's Mercedes S Class is parked there. Maybe Lannie is back to continue being her horrible self. I'm not looking forward to that. I am looking forward only to the Starbucks I know Tom will have waiting for me.

Tom is at his desk. He hands me my coffee and says, "Waiting in your office."

Before I leave him, I say, "Look in my email for something from Johnny. He's supposed to send files on everyone who works in his office. The files may help you get more and better information on his employees. Also keep after Grace's phone."

"I'm on it," he says.

I walk into my office, and who is sitting there but none other than Edgar Trumpf himself. He ignores me. He's reading a newspaper. *The Wall Street Journal*, I think. As I sit, I say, "So how are the lives of the millionaires doing today, Mr. Trumpf?"

"It's billionaires!" he says. "Millionaires are nothing. Given inflation and all. And the Fed? Everyone on the Board of Governors should be drawn and quartered. What they're doing to this country!"

"Right," I say. What a jerk he's being. Of course, I've heard of the Fed, but I don't know what it does. I'm certainly not going to ask Edgar why he's feeling murderous toward it. "What brings you in today, Mr. Trumpf?"

He's not as good-looking as he seemed the other night at the restaurant, but I didn't get a close look at him then. He needs a haircut. He should wear his hair shorter and a little fluffed up in front. While I'm thinking these things, he says, with narrowed brows, "Have you been following me?"

"What could possibly make you think I've been following you?"

"The other night at the restaurant? I saw you. Everywhere I go, I see you!"

"Sir," I say. "That is not true." In fact, it isn't true. Over the last two years, I've tailed him for a few hours maybe five, six times. He can't be seeing me everywhere he goes. Not possible.

"Look," he says, now a little calmer. "I know Lannie thinks I'm having an affair. She's thought that from the day we were married. I love her, but she's an extraordinary pain in the ass. Surely, you must see that about her. I'm not having an affair. I'm too busy working to become a billionaire, for Christ's sake! When the hell would I have time to have an affair?"

"A billionaire? Really?"

"No, not really, but something like that."

"You and Lannie have talked about this affair business?"

"Many times. Many times. I came here today thinking maybe I could get you to get her to see reason. She's not being reasonable. She's making me crazy." He picks up a pencil and begins tapping it on the desk. There's something that seems essentially decent and trustworthy about Edgar. I always trust my instincts about things like that, although I'm not sure I should. Some people who have seemed the most decent and trustworthy to me in the past have turned out to be pretty bad people. And so because of an occasional unfortunate outcome, I don't always go with the gut, but sometimes I do. I'm going with the gut with Johnny. I am with Edgar.

"There's only one thing I can suggest to you, sir," I say.

"Call me Edgar, for Christ's sake."

"Okay, Edgar, there's only one thing I can suggest." I open a desk drawer and pull out a card and hand it to him.

He reads it, "'Marial Swenson, Couples Counseling.' Are you serious, for Christ's sake?"

"I am. Look. I don't think Lannie is going to stop trying to find evidence of an affair. Your only choice, besides leaving her, is to get some help. People do it all the time. Marial Swenson is quite good. Trust me on this."

"I absolutely do not trust you on anything, and I'm certainly not going with my crazy wife to spend time with a woman shrink, for Christ's sake."

I open the desk drawer again. I pull out another card and hand it to him.

He reads it, "'Hal Marshall, Couples Counseling.' You never give up, do you?"

"Yeah, I do give up. I give up quite often. I'm your basic wimp. I suppose that's the reason I'm an investigator. I'm compensating."

"That sounds like shrink talk to me."

"I guess it kind of is, yeah." Now I'm twirling my hair. Lannie is dreary. Edgar is so dreary. These people need to get a life.

"Couples counseling," Edgar says. "What goes on in couples counseling?"

"Basically, you talk – with a third person present, who is a kind of referee – about whether or not you still love each other, whether or not you want to save your marriage, and if the answers to each of those inquiries is 'yes,' then you proceed in trying to figure out how to make each other happier. I was in couples counseling with my first husband. It was an engaging and gratifying experience."

"First husband?" Edgar says. "That implies that there was or is a second husband, so couples counseling didn't work for you."

"I'm happy to say that it did work. Those two questions I mentioned. Are you in love? Do you want to save the marriage? We both answered those questions with a 'no.'"

"I'm not up for a shrink, but I can't get divorced. It would destroy my career."

"Well, maybe that concern in itself is a

problem. Maybe Lannie thinks the only reason you come home at night is because of your career, not because of your marriage."

"You think?" He's not asking a question.

"No, Edgar. I don't think anything. This is all for you and Lannie to explore."

Edgar stands and looks at the card again. "Maybe," he says. "Do I have to pay you?"

"You do," I say. "Talk to my assistant Tom as you go out."

Now I have my feet up on my desk. I'm drinking my Starbucks. I turn on *Investigation Discovery*. I'm in heaven. But only for half an hour. Mike calls. "I have it," he says.

"Have what?"

"We have Grace's phone records. We know everyone she's talked to for the last six months. And listen to this. I called Johnny and ran by him all the names. He knew everyone except for one person. Her name is Angela McCain. She works in Melton as a bookkeeper."

"How often do Grace and Angela talk?"

"Not every day. But usually three or four times a week over the past six months."

"This is interesting. Can you text me her number," I say.

I call Angela McCain. I tell her I'm working for Grace Cheung's family, and I'm asking Grace's friends if they might know where she is. I say, "Her husband is a little worried about her. She's been gone for a couple days. Apparently, she takes off on her own once in a while. So he's not terribly worried."

"Oh," Angela says. "I'm sorry. I have no idea where she might be. I haven't spoken to Grace in a while."

"A while?" I say.

"Oh, I'd say a week or so." Angela sounds a little nervous, but maybe I'm imagining that.

"Do you have time now to talk a little about Grace?" I ask.

"Not really," Angela says. "You've caught me at work. Could we maybe meet somewhere around lunchtime?"

"Today?"

"Yes."

"Absolutely."

"Are you in Melton?" she asks.

I tell her I can be there in ninety minutes. "We can meet at noon," I say. Text me the name and address of a restaurant you like."

In the office, I always keep a small overnight bag packed and ready to go. For emergencies. I pick it up and tell Tom, "Ninety minutes to Melton. Ninety minutes back. I can't do that day after day. Make a reservation for me for tonight at the Holiday Inn in Melton. I'm sorry, but you'll have to run with the dogs tomorrow morning."

"That's fine," Tom says. "I'll call your mom and tell her I have to pick up the dogs. I know she'll invite me for dinner. She makes a killer meatloaf. I loved it last night."

"You did? You liked her meatloaf? Really?" I'm

beginning to have doubts about Tom.

Then I'm on the road. Same old road. Road to Melton. I stop at Jay's Fabulous and Amazing Pawn Shop on the way. I find a woman's steel and gold Rolex watch, but no woman's all gold Rolex. I don't think Jay is hiding anything from me because he doesn't know I'm an investigator. I give him the story about my wanting to buy a gold Rolex for my mother and give him my number. During the entire time I'm in the shop, Jay has his hands palms down resting on a glass display case counter. All his nails are bitten down past the quick, as if he spends all day, each day gnawing on his hands. The nails look odd and creepy. I feel sorry for him. How much pain does a person have to be experiencing to want to gnaw on his hands like that?

I'm back on the road and who is calling me but Leslie. "Hello, darlin'," she says. "I have to ask you for a favor."

"Anything," I say. And I soon discover that is the wrong thing to say.

"Honey, it's about my Doug. I think my Doug is foolin' around on me. So here's the scoop. He told me he has to go to Chicago for a dinner tonight. He said he'd have to spend the night at the home of some bigwig there. But guess what? I happened to be going through his email this morning. I found a reservation at the Melton Holiday Inn for tonight. He flat out lied to me. I want you to catch him in the act. Please!"

"How did you get into his computer?"

"I have his passwords. All of them. He's so transparent. And I have to find out if he's foolin' around on me. I've already started moving money out of our joint account. The bastard."

"Leslie," I say. "I have the feeling this is a misunderstanding." I'm thinking that I know Doug. Doug is as loyal as a basset hound, and he looks like one, too. Who would want to fool around with Doug? But I can't say this to his suspicious wife.

"No, honey bunch, it's not a misunderstanding. You have to help me. I'm your best friend."

"Well, it so happens I'm staying at the Melton Holiday Inn tonight. Tell me something. When does he usually leave work?"

"He told me he's leaving the office at six to drive to Chicago."

"If he's going straight to the hotel….."

"I bet he is."

"Then he'll be at the hotel around six thirty. I'll set up in the lobby and wait for him to check in. But look, don't waste my time. If he comes home, let me know. I'm sure this is a misunderstanding."

"Misunderstanding, my ass!" Leslie says.

Now it's on to Melton. The road to Melton. So boring. The next call is from Tom. He tells me he has the employee files Johnny sent, and he's studied them and finished research on everyone.

"So fast?" I say.

"Yes. Johnny gave me a lot of information. Did you know," Tom says, "that there's a law saying that if Joe Schmoe is out of work and looking for a job and a prospective employer calls Joe's former employer to ask about Joe, the former employer is legally permitted to reveal only how long Joe worked for him, what Joe's job was and what Joe's salary was? Can't say anything more. Legally, that is. Did you know that?"

"Surely that's not an Indiana law. I don't think Indiana gives a hoot what someone says about a former employee."

"Actually, Indiana does care. But that's neither here nor there. Listen to this. If you work in the securities industry as, say, a broker-dealer or an investment adviser, the rules are a lot different. Extensive background checks are required by the Feds before a financial services firm can hire anyone. Even the secretaries and admins who work in Johnny's office have been heavily background checked. And if you work in the securities industry, information and opinions about you recorded in one place of employment go with you automatically to your new place of employment. If you did a bad, you can't escape that bad and continue working in the industry. You can trust me on this: Johnny's people are all squeaky clean. Completely squeaky clean, with the exception of the one DUI I told you about before. Yup."

I thank Tom. I do think he's a gem.

Mike calls. The first thing out of his mouth is, "I'm mad at you."

"No, you're not," I say.

"I am."

"Why?"

"What you said last night about Curly and Stretch is getting to me today."

"What I said was merely something I wanted you to think about. Curly and Stretch represent penises in the unconscious mind. Your unconscious mind. My unconscious mind. It's a thought. The thought is that you feel inadequate and need extra penises around. Also, what about your misogyny?"

"You think I hate women?"

"No. You don't. So grow up. Put on your big boy pants and get rid of Curly and Stretch."

"What has not hating women got to do with Curly and Stretch? Anyway, you know, it's possible Curly and Stretch are girls."

"We have to talk about this later. You have to get rid of the snakes."

"No," he says. "No, I won't."

"Okay, dude, good-bye." What a baby.

I'm meeting Angela McCain at a place called Traylor's Bistro. Nice big parking lot in front. I stand inside the front door for a little while. Angela said she would be wearing a red hat. I see her. Her hat is large and floppy. She's already seated. As I walk toward her, she waves to me. She is a well-dressed woman who is, I'm guessing, in her late twenties. Tailored look, except for the hat, which she quickly jettisons. Delicate good looks, lots of long blonde hair, making the fact that she's named after angels seem about right. She's shakes my hand without enthusiasm, smiling a little. We order from the limited menu. After we order, Angela suddenly looks quite serious. "What is all this going on with Grace?" she says.

I tell her exactly what I told her on the phone. Grace is missing. Who knows where she could be? I ask her, "How do you and Grace know each other? Her husband says he doesn't know you?"

"Well, it's an odd story," she says. "Do you know an exclusive dress shop in Indianapolis called Sherrill's?"

I look down at my semi-shabby clothes – old black pants, shiny from wear, and a white blouse, no longer so white, under one of my mother's old, extremely old suit jackets – and say, "Do I look like someone who would know an exclusive dress shop in Indianapolis?"

Angela laughs. "Well, you may be aware of all the wonderful clothes Grace owns. We met at Sherrill's about six or seven months ago. She was looking for a winter coat, something she could travel with. But it had to be the best. Always the best with Grace. Sherrill's sometimes carries coats from a French designer who produces little, but sells in the U.S. for quite a lot of money. The day I met Grace there, she asked me what I thought about several of the designer's coats she tried on. I had to tell her, because it was true, that she looked stunning in everything she tried on. I often travel to France. My mother has a lot of family there. I told Grace I was going to Paris a week or so later, that I knew a designer there whose clothing she would love. Frederic Patton. I told her I would go to his shop in Paris and send her pictures of his clothing. I did that, and I guess that's how we became friends. When I got back to Melton, I called her. We met for lunch and immediately became friends."

"Why do you think she didn't tell Johnny about you?"

"Sometimes Johnny gives Grace trouble about all the money she spends on clothes. Clothes are her passion, really. And mine, too. More than having lunch together, we shop together. I have more clothes than I know what to do with, and so does she. We're always saying to each other, 'We have to stop this!' But we don't stop."

"Does Grace ever seem particularly depressed to you?" I ask.

"No, never," Angela says, shaking her head with what I think is disbelief that anyone would ask a question like that about Grace. "She's never been depressed that I've known about. Never."

"Do you mind telling me a little about yourself, Angela?" I say. "I'm asking all Grace's friends to answer a few personal questions for me. For example, where do you work?"

"I'm a bookkeeper for a diamond and jewelry dealer and sales house. Max's Diamonds. Have you heard of it?"

"Yes. The company advertises on TV, right?"

"Yes. Yes, they do. Quite a nice business. I've been there for about four years. I grew up in

Chicago. My parents still live there. I'm not married. About five years ago, I moved to Indianapolis to live with a boyfriend. He's now long gone. No current boyfriend. I now live in Melton with one of my four – count'em four – brothers. His name is Andrew. We only live together during the summer. He's a college student. Goes to Butler. He's smart. Wants to be some kind of engineer. That's all a bit beyond me. Science and stuff. I'm strictly a numbers girl." We both laugh. Her laugh is a little forced.

I ask Angela if she can think of anywhere Grace might have gone off to on her own.

Shaking her head, pursing her lips, she says, "I can't think of anywhere. No. She is a happily married woman. Except for one thing. She always says that Johnny thinks her passion is knitting. How wrong he is! Well, if you've seen her closet, I don't have to tell you."

After lunch, I give Angela my card. "Call if you think of anything that might be helpful."

Back in my car, I think about Angela. The discomfort in her laugh. There's something off about her. I call Mike. "Let's not talk personal right now," I say.

He agrees. I tell him about my meeting with Angela. "Something's off," I say.

"How do you mean?" he asks.

"I don't know. Maybe I'm being unduly suspicious. But it bothers me that Johnny doesn't know her. It seems odd."

Then he says, "I have an idea. I think, since

you're already in Melton, you should call Dan Tiernan and go see him. He's a good guy. And he's smart. He's someone you could talk to about police department relations with the Chinese. He's someone you should know. He's a great resource."

I call Dan Tiernan, who says he'll be happy to meet with me. I drive to downtown Melton to the police station in which he lurks. The building is old and could use a facelift. I was in this station several times in the old days when I was a cop. It hasn't changed one bit. Still the worn oak floors. Still the walls painted an awful dirty light green. I guess it has to be green. It couldn't be blue. Blue would reek of the nursery or the hospital. Yellow? No. Too provocative. So green it is. I ask for Dan at the front desk. He comes out to take me back to his office in the bowels of this atrocious building. He looks like someone sent from central casting to play a movie cop. Early fifties. Big. Gruff manner. A head of more great Irish hair than any man his age has a right to. Instead of sitting at his desk, he sits next to me in one of the two chairs in front of his desk. I'm wondering why he would do this. I pull my chair around so I'm looking more right at him.

"I guess Mike has told you about my case," I say.

"Yes, he has," he says. "And I want you to know we're looking for the Rolex."

"Well, thank you for that," I say. "If the watch were found, we'd know for sure that Grace has met with trouble."

"I have one question," Dan says. "How do you engrave a Rolex?"

I laugh. "I don't know. All I know is that it was done. Can I ask you a question?"

"Of course."

"Do you have a kind of a gut feeling about this situation?"

"My gut feeling is that this will not end well." Then he straightens up a bit, clears his throat. "But I'm not sure. Interestingly, the police, as you probably know from your years on the force, generally say reassuring things to anyone who reports a loved one is missing. Police say, 'Oh, in most cases like this, the so-called missing person shows up eventually. Don't worry too much.' That's what we say. But it's a lie."

"Is it? I don't think I ever understood that."

"That's been my experience. At first, you say only reassuring things. Then it all goes from bad to worse."

"You also know my client, Grace's husband, who is Chinese American, is insistent that he won't deal with the police. Are relations between the police and the Chinese community here so bad?"

"Yes, they're terrible," Dan says. "The Chinese hate the police. The police call the Chinese here the 'Great Wall of Silence.'"

"That's not good. I was wondering about something. Do you have any idea of how Melton came to have such a substantial Chinese community?"

Dan says, "Most of them are Christians. There was a Protestant church here for decades called The Innocent Lamb. One of the parishioners was a wealthy guy named Kapp. He gave the church a lot of money over the years, which the church used to help Chinese Christians come to America, specifically to Melton. Kapp may have specified that they use a lot of his money that way. I'm not sure. I know he believed that Christians in China don't have the easiest time. I don't think Johnny Cheung's parents came over as Christians."

"That's right," I say. "There is a Melton doctor who helped them."

"But here's something," Dan says. "I heard this guy talking on the radio about teaching policing at some big college back East. I contacted him a few days ago. His name is Ethan Welsh. I told him this department here has got a lot of money in a slush fund and that we'd like to give him that money. We hired him to come out here for a couple months and help our department try to figure out how to engage the Chinese. Convince them that we're here to help. Not to hurt. Although, honestly, given what's happened to the Chinese in the past, I don't blame them for being mistrustful. The department wants to change that."

"That sounds great. What kinds of things does this guy suggest?"

"I'm not sure what he's going to tell us. It's interesting how the issues one community faces with policing are often so different from those faced by another community. For example, Camden, New Jersey, needed budget cuts a few years ago, so the city stopped requiring its police to live in Camden. The police force became a county force. And this has caused policing to kind of go to hell there. At least that's what some people say. I don't know for sure. The idea is that if police live in the city, they know the city, they know the people. They're less like a military force and more a part of the community. But in Melton, we have exactly the opposite problem. We want our cops to live outside Melton, if at all possible. Our view is that we want to avoid conflicts of interest. We don't want our cops to be too friendly with anyone in Melton."

"But you want to improve your relations with the Chinese, so…"

"Yeah, we don't know how this guy will analyze our situation. But we think it could be a good thing if he can help us bring the Chinese into the fold, so to speak. We know there's crime in the Chinese community. Almost none of it is reported. Often there are people in that community who are living without any kind of protection. They can be victimized and have no one to turn to for help. Not everyone can afford to hire Jan March to help them with their problems. Well, I guess that's obvious."

"I'd like to hear more once this Ethan Welsh arrives."

"Leave me your card. I'll call you. You could come to some training sessions if you want to."

I tell him I'd like that. Then I ask him why

he's sitting next to me rather than across from me on the other side of his desk. "Oh," he says. "We've all recently had some sensitivity training." His index fingers make quotation marks in the air. "They don't call it that. They call it something that's more acceptable to the macho types around here, but it's sensitivity training. The trainers suggest we sit beside people who come into our offices. They say that sitting beside someone in conversation – as opposed to looking directly ahead at them – is less likely to elicit a hostile reaction. That's what the trainers say. Now, of course, you can't sit nicely next to someone if you're afraid of the person who comes into your office." Dan chuckles. His chuckles are the chuckles of the weary and worldly-wise. I like Dan Tiernan. I'm happy to know him.

After I say good-bye to Dan, I head for the Holiday Inn. I check into the hotel about four o'clock, take a nap, take a shower, then head down to the lobby with a magazine I pretend to read while I wait to see if Leslie's husband Doug checks in with a sweetie. And, well, shit! About six thirty, in walks Doug with a sweetie on his arm.

CHAPTER 9

I wake up in the late morning. I want the free hotel breakfast, so I throw on some clothes and head down to the breakfast room, hoping to get there before it closes. I turned my phone off after I saw Doug come into the hotel. I couldn't face Leslie last night. While sitting with my coffee and institutional scrambled eggs (which, for some reason, I love, maybe because they remind me of college, which I didn't like, except for the eggs), I turn on my phone and see that Leslie has called me sixteen times since last night. This kind of makes me feel like a heel. Then I think, what is a "heel," anyway? That's what women called men in 1950's movies. Yeah, that's what I feel like, some jerk in a 1950's noir film.

I call Leslie. I tell her I saw Doug with someone last night, and it looked like they were both checking into the hotel. "Leslie, I want to talk to him. Before you do anything, will you please let me talk to him? When is he supposed to be home today from his supposed trip to Chicago?"

She stops me in my tracks. She says, "First, I'm mad at you for not taking my calls last night." I tell her I'm sorry, that I was a chicken.

"Second," she says, "I'm done here. I've packed

my bags and I'm about to go out the door to my cousin's. She lives in Lakewood. Doug the dog – that's what I'm calling him now – said he would be home by noon." I can hear Leslie tapping on the phone with a fingernail. I think it's interesting that she's calling him "Doug the dog." I wonder if she knows he looks like a basset hound.

I say, "Leslie, you can leave if you want to, but I'm driving to your house to wait for Doug to come home. I'm going to talk to him."

"Yes, you do that, darlin'. Me, I'm outta here!" She hangs up.

I'm sitting in the front hotel lounge in my quasi-pajamas. I'm sitting on a sofa, not a long sofa, but, nevertheless, I decide to lie down on it. It's a lovely sofa, orange (what is it with hotels and orange?), but the fabric is soft to the touch. I lie down, then bring my arm up over my eyes and attempt to veg out. My efforts are for naught. Soon there is a man in a uniform leaning over me. "Ma'am," he says. "Are you okay?"

"I'm okay," I say. "Do I have to sit up?"

"Yes, ma'am, you do," he says. Such a nice young man. He probably doesn't yet understand how life can drain you and, when you least expect it, make you want to lie down exactly where you are.

"I'm not going to sit up," I say. "You have to give me another minute or two lying down."

"No, ma'am, I can't do that. I'm sorry. I'll have to call security."

"You have uttered the magic word," I say.

"'Security!' I'll sit up!"

I sit up and my phone rings. It's Lannie Trumpf. I don't have the courage to listen to one of her rants, but I also don't have the courage to look forward to listening to one of her rants later in the day. (Face the music, Jan. You knew this was coming.) I answer the phone while sitting knees apart, elbows on knees. "Hello, Lannie," I say. "How are you?"

"How do you think I am, you skank? You talked to my husband! You talked to my husband!! Whatever happened to your obligation of confidentiality to me, your obligation to me?" She is quite shrill, worse than ever.

"Read our contract," I say, quietly. "I think you'll find I didn't breach any legal obligation I have to you." I go on, "Lannie, I think he loves you. I trust him. You're going to lose him if you keep up this insane quest."

"Insane quest? Insane quest?"

I think it's time to take a step back. "I'm sorry. That a was bit harsh," I say. Now I'm lying down again. Well, not lying down, sort of slumping to the side. A kind of a lie. But not a true lie.

"Yes, I'd say a bit harsh. Oh, my God, he tells me you told him we should go to couples counseling. Are you crazy? Are you out of your mind? The man is boffing everything in the county, and you recommend couples counseling?"

Now all I can come up with is a whisper. "Okay, Lannie, what do you want me to do?" If she weren't paying me so much, I'd fire myself.

"I want you to get the evidence I require."

"When you have another proposed stakeout, let me know." After I hang up, I think I should have been tougher on her. But what would the point have been? She's out of her mind.

I call Mike. I tell him about my meeting with Dan Tiernan. I tell him how much I like Dan Tiernan. I tell him about Leslie and Doug. "Wait a minute," he says. "Surely, Leslie understands that Doug looks like a basset hound and that no one would want to fool around with him."

"I don't think she understands that," I say. "I'm driving up to see Doug, and then I'm heading home." I tell Mike I'm beat.

"You're in the wrong business," he says. The voice he's speaking in is somewhat snippy and know-it-all, and I don't like it. "You're too easily whipped," he adds. "Get out while you can."

"You're joking, right?" I say.

"Yeah, kind of, but not really. I have a fantasy of you at my house hanging out all day with Curly and Stretch. I come home after work to find you in an apron, putting the finishing touches on a fabulous dinner for the two of us."

"In your dreams!" I say, a little too loudly for the lounge. I have a momentary daydream. I'm in an apron, standing at the stove in Mike's house. The two boas are wrapped around my body, starting down below with my ankles and moving upward. One of them is looking straight into my eyes and is offering me an apple he has in his mouth.

"Okay, enough of that," Mike says. "Two things. The letter from Grace's parents to Johnny. It says what he said it says. It says that Grace was depressed on and off as an adolescent. Chinese doesn't contain a word for 'depression' in the Western sense."

"How can that be?" I say.

"I'm simply giving you my thoughts. To the Chinese, 'depression' is more like 'extreme sadness.' If you're Chinese you don't get depressed, I guess. I mean why would you? You're Chinese! The second thing is, I want to you to spend the night at my house tonight. I'll cook. No, I won't cook. I'll sort of cook. I'll bring food in."

I tell him I can't stay the night with him. "I have to go home to Mom tonight," I say. "We haven't spoken since we had our tiff about Jim Peterson, the slapper. I've got to talk to her. But how about tomorrow? Sunday brunch out."

"No, I'll make brunch," he says.

"No," I say. "We'll have brunch out. I'm not eating your bad cooking."

"My cooking is bad?"

"It is. I can't forgive you for putting a jar of peanut butter into that chili you made."

"You have to get over that," he says. "You have to give me another chance."

Soon I'm on the road to Dayton, to Leslie's house. I call Johnny and tell him about my meeting with Angela. I then ask him what he thinks. "I don't know what to think," he says. "This Angela person is kind of a secret friend? I don't get that."

"Angela says it's about money, that she and Grace are shopping addicts together, and Grace has to hide her shopping from you and, I guess, she has to hide the identity of her partner in crime."

"That doesn't make sense. We have a lot of money. Grace knows she can buy anything she wants. I didn't care what she spends."

"Angela says you do care what she spends."

"Not true," he says. "That's not true. Not true." He pauses. "Nothing on the Rolex? Nothing on Grace's phone?"

"Johnny, you are the first person I would call if I had any kind of clue, any kind of evidence. Surely, you must know that."

"Yes, yes," he says. "I know that."

I'm heading to Dayton. I call Leslie, who says she's on her way to her cousin's house. I tell her: "I want you to know I'm on my way to your house to meet with Doug. Did you leave him a note? He's going to be upset when he arrives home and you're not there."

"To hell with him," she says. "I didn't leave a note. I want him to hurt as much as I do."

"Oh, Leslie! Leslie!" I say. "I'll call you after I see him."

"Don't bother!"

"Of course, I'll bother. Stop being so difficult."

"I like being difficult," she says. "It suits me."

"But I'm your best friend. Don't be difficult

with me." Leslie hangs up on me.

I sit in my car in the driveway of her house. I could go in. I have keys. But I'm not sure I'm ready for Big Dog. I need a minute to prepare to meet him. After I sit and breathe deeply for a while, I'm prepared for him, and I go in, leash him up and head for Leslie and Doug's small private forest. Leslie always says, "Oh, it's only a few trees, for God's sake." But to me, it's a forest. It's late summer, the best time of year in Indiana. The air is warm, but the breeze carries a hint of the coming cooler weather. The sun pouring through the trees and the crunch of underbrush are calming to both canine and human being. We're happy. After a while, I spot Doug's car in the distance heading toward the house.

When Big Dog and I walk in the front door, Doug turns and asks, "Where is Leslie?"

"Sit down," I say. "We have to talk." Doug automatically sits. So does Big Dog. Such good boys.

Doug leans way back into the sofa. "Has my baby left me?" he asks. There is great sadness in his voice.

"Why would you think she's left you?"

"Well, she's not here. And she's been strange lately. I knew something was wrong. Who did she leave me for?" He wants to know for whom his two-hundred-pound wife has left him. Wow, does he love this woman!

I tell him Leslie hasn't left him for anyone, and that last night I saw him checking into the Melton Holiday Inn with a young woman. Doug breathes a sigh of what is obviously relief. He puts a hand over his heart. He says, "That was Adele Winthrop, my secretary. Oh, my God, what a misunderstanding! Adele came to work yesterday all beaten up. Her husband had beaten her, and then he convinced her she was fine to go to work." He shows me a picture of Adele that's on his phone. Half her face is black and blue, and one eye is swollen shut. "I took her to my lawyer's office. My lawyer is Nancy Green, and she took pictures of the bruises all over Adele's body. Then we went to Nancy's doctor, who examined Adele. Nancy's going to get a restraining order against Adele's husband. Thank God, Adele has no kids. Then the three of us went to the police station, and we filed a domestic violence complaint with Officer Dennis Crew. Call him. He'll tell you."

Doug hands me Denny's card. I call Denny, whom I know from the old days. He won't confirm that Adele Winthrop filed a domestic violence complaint yesterday. He tells me he can't talk to me about complaints or investigations. I say, "Come one, Denny, it's me, Jan! Talk to me!"

"No can do," he says. "Sorry." And he hangs up. I immediately call Mike and ask him to call Denny and find out if a complaint was filed and what the police are doing about it.

Mike calls back five minutes later and says, "Yes, the complaint was filed. And Nancy Green and Doug Faber were with Adele when she filed. Nothing is being done with the complaint. Not enough evidence to investigate."

"What are you talking about?" I say. "I'm looking at a picture of this woman's face. Her husband is clearly using her face as a punching bag!"

"Well, Denny is telling me that this guy Winthrop is a big deal, an executive at Pierce."

"Tell me you're kidding me! They won't investigate because the husband is a big deal!" I yell. "Well, we'll see that bastard in court!" Mike tells me to calm down. I tell him I absolutely will not calm down. I get off the phone and then I calm down.

Doug says, "I took Adele to the hotel last night so she would be safe. Her sister is on her way from Ohio to pick Adele up and take her back to Ohio. Adele has a lot of family there."

"Well," I say. "One good thing is that if this guy Winthrop is a big deal, he most likely won't become a stalker. Too busy climbing to the top. He'll fight the restraining order though. A restraining order is not a good thing to have on your record if you're an exec at a company like Pierce."

Doug suggests that maybe he should tell Nancy not to go for the restraining order. He says, "Nancy could call Winthrop and threaten a restraining order if he doesn't leave Adele alone. I think that threat could be quite effective."

"Do it," I say. And Doug calls Nancy.

And I call Leslie. I tell Leslie the sad tale of Adele. "Oh, thank heavens," she says. "I'm packing up right now. Tell my baby I'll be home in an hour."

I tell her baby that his wife will be home in an hour, and then I lie down on the carpet next to Big

Dog and we hug. "What are you doing?" Doug asks.

"I can't move," I say. "There's something about this dog that makes me want to never move." But, of course, eventually I do move.

I'm on the road once again, and Mike calls. He says, "Are you driving?" I say I am. "Well, pull over right now," he says.

"Why?" I say.

"Do it!" he yells. I pull over. I ask him what the hell is going on.

"You aren't going to believe this," he says. "But after you spoke to Lannie this morning, she went to her husband's office and shot him!"

"No! No! Wait!" I say. "No! Mike, say it isn't so!"

"It is so. Jesus, she's crazy! He's in the hospital. Looks like he'll be okay. She got him in the shoulder. And you know what? One good thing will come of this."

"What's that?" I ask.

"Now, unless he's completely out of his mind, he'll divorce her."

CHAPTER 10

When I get to my mom's house, I walk into the kitchen. I smell chops sizzling in a pan. We're eating in the kitchen tonight. A big salad is already on the table. The table is set for two. "You're late," my mom says. She won't look at me.

"I'm not late," I say.

"Fill the water glasses. Take the bread to the table," she orders me. I follow her orders and then sit at the table.

"I'd like a glass of wine," I say.

"You're becoming a drunk," she says.

I say, "What a thing to say! You know that's not true. But I don't have a problem with drinking water if it makes you feel more comfortable." Once we're eating, things are quiet again, but she still won't look at me. I want to talk. I say, "What do you think about the fuss about the name Sutterton?"

"What about it?"

"Some people want to change the name because…."

"I know all that. Who cares?" She still won't look at me. "John Sutter was a Christian man. Why would anyone in California want to blacken his name? I don't get it."

"He abused indigenous people."

"Really? You mean he called them 'Indians'?" She is not being my mom tonight. This attitude is not one I've seen before."

"Mom, you know it was more than that."

Finally, she looks at me. But there is a large, mean, sad frown on her face. "Oh, I know you're right. But I have to tell you, after our argument about Jim Peterson, I am wondering whether you're a Christian woman."

"Why are we talking about this now?" We've talked about this before, but not often, and always in reasonable terms. Why is my mother suddenly so interested in my beliefs and in such a super-charged way?

"Maybe because of Jim," she says. "Our argument."

"What has our argument about Jim have to do with whether or not I'm a Christian?"

"I like him, Jan. He's a good Christian man. It occurs to me that the story he told me about his daughters not liking me is an excuse, and that he no longer wants to see me because he thinks you're not a believer."

I'm stunned. The dogs can sense something is wrong. They come to my side, as if to protect me. Their nervous systems are on high alert. I say, "Mom, did you ask Jim about this?"

"Not yet. I've been thinking. But tell me, please, that you believe in God. So when I talk to Jim, I can tell him that my daughter is a God-fearing soul."

Because I love my mother, or at least I think I do (haven't examined that issue in a while), I say, "Of course, Mom. Of course, I believe in God." I should have stopped there. I had a win. But no. I had to continue. "Mom, Jim hit you. That's an issue that I, for one, am not going to let you ignore."

She waves me away with one hand. "Oh, that was nothing. Belief is everything. Little slaps are nothing!" I think my mom is losing it.

I leave her. I go to my room. I feel like a banished adolescent. The situation reminds me of the time my father quoted Kingsley Amis, who when once asked if he believed in God, said, "Yes, I do believe in Him, and He has a lot to account for." I chuckle. Then I sleep. I dream of my father, which makes sense in a way, because when he was alive he often soothingly kept my mother from veering into extreme religiosity. Whenever my mother was moving in that direction, you generally knew it because she would start hammering away about how someone – always a different person each time – was not spiritual enough for her. In my dream, my father is walking along as he did in life, bent slightly forward due to an old college football injury. But his hair looks messy, and he has deep, dark circles under his eyes. He's not the dapper guy he was when he walked the Earth. He looks at me and smiles and tells me not to worry so much.

I awaken in the dark and think about my father's once telling me that Freud believed that the unconscious mind has no understanding of death. To the unconscious mind, someone who is dead is not dead (since there is no death). An actually dead person is, to the unconscious mind, simply gone, that is to say, simply not present. It is only with our conscious minds that we can grasp the reality of someone's death. Since dreams waft up from the unconscious mind, how lucky we are that our deceased loved ones can appear in our dreams as very much alive. A small respite from the unending pain of loss.

I sleep again. I dream of Grace walking in Leslie and Doug's forest. I stand at the edge of the forest, but I can't walk toward Grace. All I can do is yell at her, "Grace! Grace!" She can't hear me. She begins to walk toward me, but doesn't respond to my calls. Once she's close to me, she reaches out to me and says, in a soft voice, almost a whisper: "No love to die for."

I awaken. What was Grace talking about? I should know. It's my dream, after all. I constructed it. What am I trying to tell myself?

In the morning, I decide I have to push Grace aside for a while. I drink coffee with my mother, who is not speaking to me. I run with the dogs and then load them into my car and head to Mike's house. I call him from the car to tell him I'm bringing the dogs, and Curly and Stretch had better be in their cages when we arrive.

Mike is cooking as Tam and Bud and I walk in. "I thought I said, 'no cooking'," I say.

Mike says, "Jan, you will love this. My specialty. Eggs benedict."

I sit and the dogs sit with me, then climb onto my lap. It's awkward, two dogs on a lap. The house is a mess. Stuff sitting all over the kitchen table. I push the dogs down and start cleaning off the table, then wonder where does all this junk go? "You need a wife," I say. "You're so messy."

"No, I don't need a wife, thank you very much," Mike says.

I ask him if he can tell me that Lannie's been arrested. "She has," he says. "And she's lawyered up, of course. She shouldn't have shot him on a Saturday because she won't be arraigned, and bail won't be set for her, until tomorrow morning. No court on the weekend. She sits in jail as we speak."

I say, "You know what I always say: 'Shoot 'em on a Monday.' More efficient that way."

Mike finishes cooking and arranging the eggs, and we sit and eat. Tam and Bud are being good. They don't beg. They lie quietly in the sun. "Mike, there are a couple of things I want to talk to you about," I say.

"Yeah?"

"Yeah. I was thinking about how I had to depend on you yesterday to get info out of Denny Crew about the battery complaint. And I was thinking about how I depend on you for so many things, professionally speaking. Maybe I'm not cut out for this work if I can't get along on my own without leaning on you two or three times a day."

"No. No," Mike says, holding his hand up to stop me talking "You're being ridiculous. You're so good at what you do. You're incredibly dedicated. You care. That is ninety-nine percent of the job. And, hey, if for some reason you couldn't rely on me, there are at least a dozen cops that I know would be more than happy to have you rely on them."

I'm surprised by what he's said. "Well, thank you for that," I say.

"No need to thank me. It's simply the truth."

We continue to eat in silence. While Mike's house is messy on the inside, it's a beautiful house. It has tall uncurtained windows. Along the front of the house, there are four in a row that look out onto rolling green hills. The day is turning into something magnificent, all warmth and blue skies. The eggs benny is not half bad. I ask, "Did you put peanut butter in the Hollandaise?"

"Very funny," he says. "But the eggs are good, aren't they?"

"They are," I say. We're quiet. Then I say, with some hesitation, "I have to ask you something." Then I tell him about my mother's religious issue with me. I say, "I don't know if I can continue to live with her. She was so intensely at me about my beliefs. I'm thinking maybe Tam and Bud and I could live with you for a while."

Mike looks away from me. Hesitates. Then he says, "For a while?"

I say, "Maybe more than a while. I think maybe you and I should give 'us' a try. What do you say?"

He says, "Jan, you know how much I like you. I think you're great." Then it's blah, blah, blah. I'm not hearing him. Then I am hearing him. He's saying, "But I'm not in love with you. I don't want to live with someone I'm not in love with. For me, it's still Belinda. I'm sorry."

Then I say, stupidly, "But Belinda left years ago."

He says, "I think maybe I'm a one-woman guy. I want to continue to work with you, of course." More blah, blah, blah. I don't hear a lot of it.

"Oh," I say. "I'm disappointed. I thought we had something. Then I thought we didn't have something. Then I thought we did. I got mixed up. I appreciate your honesty."

He says, "I think you should try to put things back together with your mom. She's basically a good person."

"Is she? Really?" I say. "I'm not sure. I don't think I can live with her right now. I can stay in the guesthouse-slash-office." Then Mike goes on with the blah, blah, blah. I leave.

I drive home feeling like I'm unraveling. I didn't understand how much I like Mike. Maybe love Mike. I drive with a heart that hurts. I start thinking about how long it will be before my heart stops hurting. A day? A week? It's physical pain, not emotional pain. Something in the body, not the mind. It's been a while since my heart has hurt like this. And my mom. I'm losing my mother, and that hurts, too. In the same place, center of the heart.

I'm thinking I'm going to be nice to my mom when I enter the house with Tam and Bud. She's sitting in the enormous living room watching something on the small TV. Big room, little TV has always seemed an odd arrangement to me, but she likes it. She acts like she doesn't see me come in, which is fine with me. After a while, I come downstairs with my suitcase. "I'll be staying in the guesthouse-slash-office," I say. "I'll take the dogs with me."

My mother says, "Don't even think about cooking in the guesthouse. That kitchen is too old."

"That's not true," I say. "I bought the stove and the refrigerator last year and had the electrical wiring redone. You know that."

"Whatever," she answers. Whoa! So mean.

Monday morning. I wake up in the bed in one of the bedrooms in the guesthouse-slash-office. Tom is standing over me. "What are you doing sleeping here?" he says. "I didn't know where you were when I came in this morning. I had to run the dogs. I'm all sweaty. And oh, my God, did you know that Lannie Trumpf shot her husband?"

"I know all about it," I say. "Take a shower. I'm going out to get us some breakfast." I throw on some clothes. I take the dogs with me and bring back McMuffins and coffee.

Tom has showered and put on clean clothes. "What are we doing today?" he asks.

I tell him I think we'll do phone interviews

with the people who work in Johnny's office. "But I did the research," Tom says. "Everyone is squeaky, as I told you."

"Yeah," I say. "But something's up. I had a dream about Grace. We have to keep at it." I look like crap, but I don't care. I head to my desk and call Johnny. I tell him the plan for the day, to talk to his employees. He's down with that. I tell Tom we'll split up the employees. He'll talk to some. I'll talk to some.

Tom is excited. "You're trusting me to do this!" he says.

I start calling. The first person I speak with is Fred Wakeman, an investment adviser. He tells me he knows little about Grace and knows nothing about the relationship between Grace and Johnny. He's never noticed things amiss between them. He's never spent personal time with Grace and Johnny. He's never been to their house. As far as he's concerned, Johnny's office runs like clockwork. He has no complaints. Employees two and three tell pretty much the same story. Oh, my God, this is boring! What is it with people who work in finance? No personality. None.

Tom comes to my desk and says he's getting nowhere with his calls. "They're all boring, right?" I say.

"Roger that," Tom says. We both laugh. "Nothing flexible about these personalities. Tight-lipped. Maybe those are the kind of people who are attracted to that kind of work, financial stuff."

"Yeah," I say. "Financial stuff!" We laugh

again. I tell Tom that a lot has happened to me personally in the last few days. I tell him I'm feeling overwhelmed. I want him to go home. I'm closing the office for the rest of the day. He's such a good guy. He says he doesn't like leaving me on my own.

"Please don't worry about me, Tom," I say. "I'll lock the door behind you." Off he goes, reluctantly. I lock the door.

In order to distract myself, I pick up Balzac's *Cousin Bette*, which I'm about half way through. The novel is a story about the poor cousin of a family that's super-rich. The richies treat their poor Cousin Bette like crap. She is planning revenge. I'm rooting for her, though I'm not sure why. The richies are mean, but Bette is also pretty mean. We'll see. It'll be a lot more pages before I know if Bette wins or loses. I nap. I sleep the deep sleep of the lonely and unloved. No dreams.

I wake to my cell phone ringing. It's Mike. I ignore the call. He calls again. I ignore him again. But he won't give up, so I answer. All he says is, "Turn on your TV. Channel 2. Local news." Then he hangs up. My first thought is why is everyone always hanging up on me? Leslie. Denny Crew. Now Mike. Is there something about me that invites hang-ups? I'll have to consider this issue later.

I turn on the TV to the local news. One person has been abducted in a multi-story parking garage in Melton. Two others, who attempted to interfere with the abduction, have been shot and killed by the abductors. There are three eye-witnesses. A pretty woman is standing on the street with a microphone in her hand. She turns and indicates the parking garage behind her. She says, "About two hours ago, on the third floor of this garage, two people, Marshall Dienst and Cheri McLynn, were shot and killed while attempting to stop the abduction of a young woman who has now been identified as Angela McCain. The abduction of Ms. McCain was successfully completed by two men who witnesses say were wearing masks and driving a white van. Those who came to Ms. McCain's assistance and were killed were perfect strangers to her, simply trying to help an innocent woman who was being assaulted."

CHAPTER 11

The next morning, I call Dan Tiernan, hoping to find out what he knows about the abduction. I can't get through to him. I leave message after message for him before I realize the two murders and an abduction the night before are most likely taking up all his time.

I call Mike to find out what he knows. I'm thinking, so Mike is not in love with me. I have to get over that some time. Mike tells me Angela's body was found early this morning about 4:00 a.m. "Found by accident," he says. "Out past Route 21. A hunter found her a little ways off the road. Two bullets to the back of the head. Jesus! What a world!"

A little later, Johnny calls. I confirm to him that the woman who was abducted was indeed Grace's friend, Angela. I don't tell him that Angela's body has been found. Things are happening too fast. I'm not sure how much to tell him. I say I'll let him know as soon as I find out if there's a connection between Grace's disappearance and Angela's abduction.

Tom arrives. He has coffee. I need coffee. I tell him what's happening. He goes to his desk. I go to mine. Next thing I know, Tom comes into my office accompanied by a young man. Tom says, "This is Angela McCain's brother Andrew. I knew you'd want to see him right away."

"Andrew," I say. "Please sit down." He's so upset that he's trembling, badly dressed. His face is puffy with misery. "You haven't had breakfast," I say.

Tom says, "We have a whole McMuffin we can give you, Andrew."

Andrew says, "I drove here from Melton because I didn't know what else to do. The police came to my house last night, after Angela was taken. A few days ago, Angela told me she'd met you. She had your card. She was upset after she talked to you. She told me you told her Grace had disappeared. She was frightened about that."

"Why do you think she was frightened?" I ask.

"Angela thought Grace's disappearance might somehow be related to her relationship with Grace."

"What could the connection be? They were friends, but so what?"

"Friends?" Andrew says. "No. They were lovers. They were madly in love. Grace was planning to leave her husband for Angela."

"Oh, my God," I say. "Now a few things are starting to make sense. Did Angela think that Grace's husband had something to do with Grace's disappearance?"

"No, she didn't. I mean, as far as we knew, Grace's husband didn't know about the relationship between Angela and Grace."

"Well, who knew about the relationship besides you?"

"Only a few people," Andrew says. "Angela told me a few people at her workplace knew. Maybe even Angela's boss, Max, the big diamond dealer. He's such a jerk! Where do you think my sister is? Why would somebody do this to her? Do you think her abduction has something to do with Grace? I'm confused. I want my sister back."

I don't know what to say to Andrew. I feel like I need reinforcements. I call Mike. I tell him that Angela McCain's brother is in my office, and I ask him to come here as soon as he can. He says, "I'm five minutes out."

Before Mike arrives, I ask Andrew if his parents know what's going on. "My parents are both dead," he says.

"Oh," I say. "Angela told me they are alive and kicking. Living in Chicago. I wonder why she would say that."

"Angela is gay," Andrew says. "Because of that, over the course of her life, she's hidden so much. She hides. Lies come out of her easily. Not with me, though. She and I are close. She never lies to me. She practically brought me up."

"She told me you and she have three brothers."

"No," he says. "That's a lie. I wish we did have three brothers. I could use them right now. But I am utterly and completely dependent on Angela. She's all I have."

Mike rushes in. Slams shut the door to the room where Andrew and I are sitting. He looks harried, like he hasn't slept. Mike ignores me and introduces himself to Andrew. He looks at Andrew, as if with curiosity. He says, "Andrew, what have you been told about your sister?"

"Not much," he says. "My sister has been taken by a couple of creeps. What do you know? Do you know anything more?"

Mike steps up to the plate without hesitation, which is perhaps the best way to step up under these circumstances. "I'm sorry to have to tell you this, Andrew, but your sister's body was found this morning. She'd been shot."

"But she's not dead, right?" Andrew says.

"I'm sorry, Andrew," Mike says. "She is dead." Then a prolonged, high-pitched cry emanates from Andrew. I recognize this cry from my policing days as the wail inevitably heard from anyone suddenly and surprisingly bereft of a great love. Mike and I rush to hug and hold up Andrew who has fallen off his chair. Tom comes in and joins us. We four stay in a kind of hugging heap for a long time. Andrew is wailing.

The wailing subsides. Andrew says, "Who did this? Who would do this?" Then he says to Mike, "Tell me you'll catch them. Tell me you will!"

"I will," Mike says. "I will. I promise."

Tom goes into the front room and brings back a McMuffin for Andrew. Andrew reaches for it clumsily, robotically, probably because he can't think of anything else to do. He takes a bite of the McMuffin and sets it on my desk.

I ask Andrew if there's anyone he can stay with for a while. I tell him I don't think he should be alone. He agrees. He calls a friend in Melton. I tell him I'll drive him there in his car. We decide Tom will follow in my car.

Before we leave, Mike and I go outside to talk. I tell him Grace and Angela were having an affair. He rolls his eyes. "Ah, things begin to fall into place. Right?"

"Right," I say.

Mike becomes intense. He runs his hands over his mouth. He's quiet, in thought for a while. Then he says, "I think Johnny's mom knew about Angela. Remember when we interviewed her, and she kept yelling, 'Tell them about the other one'? You and I originally thought she was wanting Johnny to tell us about another friend of Grace's, one he hadn't already told us about. He later denied that's what she meant. But I think 'the other one' was Angela."

"You think Johnny's mom knew about Angela and Grace?"

"I do. I do think she knew. And I think she told Johnny. She wanted Johnny to tell us about Angela. But he wouldn't. If he had, we might have been able to save Angela. Damn it!"

"Take it easy, Mike. Calm down. I'm not sure we could have saved Angela. Anyway, it's too late now."

"Okay," he says. "I think this means that

Johnny clearly was involved in the grave harm that has come to two, three, maybe four people."

"Mike, please take it easy. Please. I'm going to take Andrew to Melton, and then I'm going to hunt down Dan Tiernan. Let's not jump to conclusions without his input."

Mike says, "Okay. Okay. But call me right away after you talk to Dan." I leave him.

The drive to Melton seems especially long and painful. At one point, Andrew says, "How am I going to bury my sister? I don't have any money."

"Don't worry about that," I say. "I can take care of that. I have a trust fund for that purpose."

"To help people with funerals?" Andrew says. He looks at me like I'm a weirdo.

"No," I say. "To help people with whatever."

"It's nice that you have that," Andrew says.

"It is," I say. "It's also possible that Angela has some money saved."

"She does. But I think it'll be a little while before I can get to it. Then I can pay you back for the funeral."

I tell Andrew that once I'm back in Sutterton I'll call Carlson's Funeral Home. They'll be in touch with him. They'll take care of everything.

Andrew says, "I can't believe I'm talking about my sister's funeral. This time yesterday, she was alive and fine."

Once we're in Melton, there's a long curving road we have to take to reach Andrew's friend's house. Tom is driving close behind me. He hasn't missed a beat. I say good-bye to Andrew and give him his car keys. I join Tom in my car. "We're going to the Melton police station," I say. "I know the way."

Tom and I enter the hideous building housing the Melton police force. I ask the woman at the front desk if I can please see Dan. She says he's out. I say, "Call him. Tell him I'm here, and I'm not leaving until I see him."

She does as I ask. Turns out Dan is not out after all. He appears and walks Tom and me to his office. We all sit. Dan runs his hands over his face several times, then pulls his chair close to his desk. "I know why you're here," Dan says. "Angela. Grace. Right?"

"Right," I say. "Anything you can give me that I can tell my client, Grace's husband? Anything?"

"Well, we know that Grace's disappearance and Angela's murder are related. We arrested a guy this morning. A thug named Dibby Holloway. Stupid name, Dibby. He was arrested at that diner out past 21. Our witnesses to Angela's abduction described in detail a large tatoo that Dibby has on his left hand. Dibby fell apart right away this morning. He's told us that he and his pal were hired by Max Herrington, Angela's boss, to get rid of Grace. The disappearance of Grace was supposed to scare Angela."

"Scare Angela?" I say. "How? Why?"

"Angela was shaking down Max. She was cooking his books for him. She wanted him to pay her to keep her from reporting him to the IRS. He didn't like that. He knew about her relationship with

Grace. He thought – demented asshole that he is – that getting rid of Grace would frighten Angela, get her back in line. This guy Holloway says that he and his pal were high when they abducted Grace and killed her. He was so high that he doesn't remember where they left Grace's body." Here Dan stops. He's having a hard time.

I say, "I couldn't save Grace. And I won't even be able to bring her body home."

"No," Dan says. "I'm sorry. After they killed Grace, Max hired Holloway and his pal to take Angela and kill her, too. Holloway says he wasn't high when he killed Angela. He's filled with remorse about Angela. No remorse about Grace because he can't remember anything. His partner has fled to Ohio. We'll get him before long. Max is right now being arrested at his large and elegant home. This will all be on the news tonight. What a horrible story. Makes you wonder about the human race."

EPILOGUE

I attend Angela's funeral ten days later. She was a good Catholic woman, loyal to the Church. Yet her priest Father Grady was not initially eager to permit the burial of her body in consecrated ground because of all the scandal surrounding her death. At one point, Andrew said to me, "As if my sister asked to be gay. As if she asked to be killed." My trust fund can speak when it has to, and it spoke loudly and clearly to Father Grady, who finally agreed to officiate at Angela's funeral and agreed to the burial of her body in consecrated ground.

I also attend Grace's funeral. Her parents are Christians, Protestants, so Johnny arranges for Grace to have a Christian funeral. Although her body has not been found by the time of her funeral, she has a gravesite and a gravestone. Her children attend the funeral and are too young to display an appropriate attitude. I feel sorry for them. All I can think is that they shouldn't be here. They seem entirely confused by the proceedings. Johnny attempts to give a eulogy, but all he can say before he must stop speaking is, "Thank you for coming...."

A week goes by after Grace's funeral. Then two weeks. Then three. My mother asks me to move back into the big house with her. She says she now believes that Jim has broken off his relationship with her, not because of my spiritual failings, but because, as he originally told her, his daughters think she is "too, too." I haven't moved back in with her yet because I kind of like living in my guesthouse-slash-office. I like eating all my meals out. During the week, Tom brings me breakfast, usually a McMuffin, when he comes to work. I've gained five pounds on the McMuffins, so I know that has to stop soon. Searching for an apartment for myself might not be a bad idea.

Mike has called me. He wants to have dinner and talk. I told him I don't think I'm ready to talk yet. He's okay with that. I wonder a bit what it would be like to continue to depend on him professionally even though we're not in any other way involved.

Oh, and Leslie called me yesterday. She told me she's decided to go to a fat farm. "They tell me I can lose twenty pounds a week in this program," she says. Twenty pounds a week seems extreme to me, but she's committed.

Today I get a call from Harvey Lipton, the guy at the State Department in Chicago. "Harvey," I say. "Great to hear from you. How are you?"

"I'm doing well," he says. "I have some good news for you, Jan."

"Great," I say. "I could use some. There hasn't been a whole lot of good news around my neck of the woods lately. You know about Grace Cheung?"

"Yes, I do," he says. "Yes, I do. Very sad. But

I'm calling, as I said, with good news. Grace's brother Terry Wong has been released from prison in China. The CIA negotiated a deal for his release. As we speak, Terry is on a plane from Beijing to San Diego. The FBI will pick him up when he lands and drive him to his parents' house. He's safe in the U.S., but he can't go back to China. Ever. That's part of the terms of the deal. He has to be a good boy. I thought because of what happened with Grace, you might want to be the one to tell Johnny Cheung and Grace's parents about this. I've emailed the details to you."

I'm taken aback. I say, "How kind and generous of you to allow me to tell them. Thank you. Thank you."

"You're welcome," Harvey says.

"But tell me something, Harvey," I say. "How come we get to talk about this on the phone? How come I didn't have to come to your offices before you could tell me about Terry?"

Harvey says, "I'm sure there's no security on this call, Jan. But Terry's free, and he's on an American aircraft in the air over the Pacific. So right now I don't give a damn if the Chinese are listening in. Listen away!"

I laugh, hang up. I put my feet up on my desk. The next thing I do is call Johnny.

www.ingramcontent.com/pod-product-compliance
Lightning Source LLC
Chambersburg PA
CBHW070341130626
46556CB00007B/2965